T0319215

MY FATHER'S SONG
(Papa Ayivi's Song)

EFO KODJO MAWUGBE

 AFRAM PUBLICATIONS (GHANA) LTD.

Published by:
Afram Publications (Ghana) Limited
P.O. Box M18
Accra, Ghana

Tel: +233 302 412 561, +233 244 314 103
Kumasi: +233 322 047 524/5
E-mail: sales@aframpubghana.com
                 publishing@aframpubghana.com
Website: www.aframpubghana.com

First Published, 2015
ISBN: 9964 70 539 5

Dedication

Sefakor Abla Mawugbe

Acknowledgement

The entire Mawugbe family for adding this song to their repertoire and had time to sing it for it to be recorded. Paul Lemonye who felt this piece could never sit on the shelf but has to be published. Dora Buandoh, Ossei Agyeman, Prof. Kwabena Osei-Boahene, and Rev. Helena M-Hooper (Hoops) who had time to re read this story. Prof. Kofi Awoonor, who always challenged me to write an Ewe book or even tell an Ewe story, hope you will smile whererever you are...

I have scattered songs in numbers
Songs of joy and songs of pain,
And my heart hath often whispered
"Wilt thou find them once again?"

From INSCRIPTION, by Egbert Martin,
a 19th Century Guyanese poet.

PAPA AYIVI

Papa Ayivi was a gifted Ewe folk music composer and singer
who lived and worked as a laundry man at the then Kumasi
College of Technology (Kwame Nkrumah University of
Science and Technology) from the 1950s through the 90s.
He performed his songs mostly at funerals and other social
gatherings among members of the Togolese community
domiciled in Kumasi.

One such song, which gained much popularity and was
loved by most people in Kumasi, Accra, and Lome, was a
folk tune that told a story about an ingrate. The transcribed
and embellished lyrics of that song is what now constitute
"Papa Ayivi's Song" to the memory of a great folk music
artist.

FIRST LEG

*Akpɔkplɔ be menyakpɔna
ganyakpɔna o, eyata ne yetso,
yetsɔa yetɔ kpana.*

(The frog says it is not easy to
recover what you have lost, that
is why she carries her husband on
her back.)

As far as people of Sakabo can recollect, the village hunter by name Klogo had no relations living abroad who might have been kind enough to extend a hand of generosity to lift him out of the quicksand-like pit of poverty he had wallowed in from time immemorial. It is also a known fact that he had not come into some fortune by going to the hinterland to work in the underground mines or to fell timber. He had no known distant or close relative who might have died and bequeathed to him any tangible or verifiable inheritance.

In the view of the people of Sakabo, Klogo the hunter was numbered among the wretched of the earth and the poorest of the poor. His most treasured inheritance that everybody could testify to was the old German-made double-barrelled rifle bequeathed him by his grandfather, Agbovi, who had inherited it first from his own father Logosei Dzienyo, the legendary hunter whose feat in the jungle was still revered by both the young and the old of Sakabo.

This great grandfather of his, according to the stories making the rounds in Sakabo, was a very trusted African servant who loyally served a handle-bar-mustached-German explorer-cum-Christian missionary by name Henkel, who worked for the Bremen mission in Sakabo and its environs. Those were the days when Europe scrambled to partition Africa for the various Western European royal houses. The rifle was a gift from the German to his trusted African friend, which had been carefully preserved and passed on from one generation to the next.

As Sakpli the village drunkard often put it whenever he had had more than his fair share of *sodabi*, the local brew,

"One fine day, before the first village cock could crow, and before the village woke up from its sleep, and anyone could utter a word of meaningful morning greetings to his neighbour, a poor hunter found himself mysteriously wallowing in wealth. His status had changed. However, he would not explain his sudden rise to wealth to anybody. Nevertheless I, Sakpli, with my huge pair of ears, can hear a lot. It is not everything I hear that I can repeat, but one day I shall speak and that day rich men will come tumbling down from the comfortable saddles of their high horses. That day everyone will know that I am indeed Sakpli, the man with the satellite ears."

No one paid any attention to the effusions of a village drunkard. Many were those who believed he spoke out of jealousy, for deep down in his heart, they suspected he wished he were in Klogo's wealthy position and enjoying all the adulations heaped upon the hunter. Klogo began to receive invitations from far and near to attend naming ceremonies of babies whose parents or families he had no blood relations with. He was usually the guest of honour during important funerals and wedding ceremonies. His ankles, arms and wrists were often bedecked with bands of crafted gold ornaments that bore symbols and motifs drawn from the folklore of his people. On his feet he wore sandals whose straps were made of gold. He always made sure he arrived after all other invitees had taken their seats. No wonder someone once likened him to the sun and remarked, "Wherever Klogo appears in his wealth, the poverty of darkness has to flee." The mystery surrounding how he had come to acquire his wealth soon became the talk of Sakabo. The stirrings in the rumour mill, obviously tongue-powered and driven by Sakpli, soon churned out various accounts, some of which were outlandishly childish to explain Klogo's wealth to any willing ear.

One story had it that the hunter had gone for *akpase* or juju-money with that part of his body that pipes the tadpoles of procreation. Some said he stumbled upon a pot of gold in the forest during a hunting expedition. There was that other story making the rounds that the hunter shot a strange bird flying in the sky during a hunting expedition. When the bird hit the ground and the hunter went for it, the wounded bird pleaded for compassion and in return directed the hunter to a nearby thicket where he found a pot of gold, which transformed his life completely. Strangely enough, the young and beautiful women of Sakabo did not seem bothered in the least about the origin of Klogo's wealth. Their major preoccupation was driven by an unflinching determination to work their way surreptitiously, by any means possible, foul or fair, into the hunter's life and become bona fide beneficiaries of his

4

wealth.

Little wonder some of these young women sometimes went beyond their means to appear in expensive clothes just to attract the attention of the wealthy hunter. These women would contrive to catch Klogo's eye at any gathering where he was, as usual, the special guest.

One of such girls was Axɔlushi from the fishing community at the coast who in spite of her voluptuousness still insisted on making herself more visible to Klogo. She had gone to a local money-lender to borrow money to sew a new dress and had acquired a new set of locally-made leather sandals with imitation gold trimmings to attend a function where Klogo was going to play the role of chairperson. She had also managed to get assigned the role of the one to give the vote of thanks at the end of the function.

She had sworn to her friends that she was going to use that singular opportunity not only to work her way into Klogo's heart, but also to melt it like shea-butter under the tropical sun. She had obtained the help of the Head of the local Primary School at Akpadikɔfe, fifty-five kilometers away, to prepare the vote of thanks speech for her. It had taken her ten market days to rehearse it to perfection.

On the D-day, it turned out that it was Akuyovi, Klogo's wife, rather than the man himself who was chairing the function. The hunter had another engagement elsewhere. To make matters worse, there at the entrance to the venue stood the money-lender!

Initially Akuyovi, by virtue of her upbringing, not to mention the instructions she and her peers had imbibed during confinement as part of the puberty rites that ushered young girls from adolescence into adulthood, would have nothing to do with her husband's wealth. She felt until its source, which Klogo has deliberately allowed to remain shrouded in mystery had been fully disclosed, she was not going to have anything to do with it. She knew who she was. She knew the values of her family. One of the cardinal principles she had learnt from Saganago, her grandmother whom she had lived with since infancy because her parents died mysteriously a few weeks after her birth, was that "a man's wealth is measured by the smell, density and colour of the sweat that flows down his brows. Any wealth that a man has, without real sweat, is bound to bear the bitter fruits of sorrow and tears of agony in the long run." This axiom of Saganago's has been so ingrained in her psyche that there was no way she would abandon it for any other precept, not even for the love of her husband.

One night in bed, through gentle but careful and persistent persuasions bordering a little bit on emotional blackmail, she succeeded in getting Klogo to agree finally to reveal to her the source of his wealth the following day during supper. Akuyovi, by this act, had effectively applied one of the many tactics she learnt from Saganago: "Nothing is impossible to accomplish in this world. With tact and diplomacy, you can insult a hunchback and still get him to allow you to play free of charge with the burden he carries on his back."

That had been Saganago's favourite statement whenever people complained to her about insurmountable challenges confronting them in life. As far as she was concerned, the word 'impossibility' must not be allowed to be part of one's personal vocabulary. However, what broke Klogo's heart was Akuyovi's response after he had divulged the secret to her. "How can Alegeli, the rat, offer you all that amount of wealth? Go tell that to the fishes in the Anyako Lagoon or the nursery kids at the village abɔdzokpo."

Klogo was shocked.

"I knew you wouldn't believe me even before I told you." said he, exasperatedly.

"How do you expect me or anyone in their right mind to believe this… this… fable?" Her voice was rising.

"Oh, so you call it a fable," he said, very softly.

"Perhaps, you have a better name for it. Let me hear it", her voice rising to a higher pitch.

"I see", he intoned, as if to himself and shook his head.

"What is it that you see?" She threw her hands recklessly into the air right in front of her husband.

"It is for this very reason that I never wanted to disclose the source of my wealth to anyone in the first place. Besides, it isn't every encounter a hunter has in the forest that he comes home to share and boast about."

"I am not anyone. I am your wife. I am the one who cooks the meal you eat daily in this house. I am the one who lies next to you every night and keeps your bed and body warm. I am the

one whose waist beads you've been fondling whenever…"
Akuyovi was in full rage and spoke with such firmness that
it made Klogo wonder if his wife was not getting possessed
by some strange deity.

"I know all that but…"

"But what, my husband? Are you implying, as a wife, I am
not supposed to seek explanation to the things that don't add
up in my mind because they are coming from my husband?"

"Not that, but…"

"Or is it a desecration of some time-honoured tradition or
custom of our forefathers when I seek to know the mystery
surrounding my own husband's quantum leap from a pit of
grinding poverty on to an enviable plinth of wealth?"
Akuyovi was panting.

"You don't seem to be getting my point…" It was obvious
Klogo was getting irritated.

"And that point is?" Akuyovi cut in, throwing all caution to
the wind. Klogo paused for a while, studied the countenance
of his wife with utter astonishment and sighed heavily.

"No one is saying a tradition or custom is infringed when
you seek answers to questions. However, a trust is breached
when you cast such doubts on the truth supplied by your
husband in response to the questions you seek answers to."
He picked the bowl of water nearby and began to wash his
hands.

"What are you doing… washing your hands?" Klogo did not
dignify his wife's question with an answer but continued to
wash his hands. He reached for a napkin and wiped them dry.

"Oh I see. So, you are angry, aren't you? You are angry

Efo Kodjo Mawugbe

because I have asked you questions...Am I to understand that a good wife must not desire to know the source of her own husband's wealth? Is that what you are saying?"

Klogo did not hear his wife's last statement. He had crossed the compound and was almost shutting the gate behind him. "And you are going out!" she screamed, hurling her words at the wind, hoping they would be wafted along to reach him. Unfortunately, the words seemed to bounce back to her as the gate swung shut, like a formidable barrier between them. Akuyovi made a dash towards the gate, her voice tearing through the quietness of the evening.
"You think I don't know where you are going. I know you are going to meet Axɔlushi at the beach. That k-legged bullfrog newfound girlfriend of yours with lips like an over-used *akpledatsi*... You think I do not know there is something going on between you and her? I hear things...

People in Sakabo talk a lot... Remember she is only in your life today because of your wealth... and not because she loves you..." It suddenly occurred to her that the target of her remonstrations was nowhere in sight and should anyone just step in to find out why she was screaming, she might look stupid. With wounded pride and suppressed anger, she turned round and went back to pick the bowls containing the leftover meal and started moving towards the kitchen. Pausing at the entrance to the kitchen, she looked back at the gate her husband had walked through and sighed heavily.

"Hmmmmm...The things wealth can do to men. It blocks their ears and they no longer hear when their wives cry. I pray it doesn't enter his head to turn his brain upside down", she muttered to herself as she entered the kitchen. Having put everything in order in the kitchen, she brought out a low stool and sat under the akukɔ tree at the center of the compound, very close to the hand-dug cistern. With her right elbow planted firmly on her right thigh and her chin cupped in the palm of her right hand, she gazed into the gray evening skies, as if to divine what the future held for her in her tottering marriage to a hunter. She sat quietly and pondered over the tiff she had had with him. Can a lighthearted altercation such as they had just had be a genuine cause for going away from home? She wondered.

As far as she was concerned, she had not behaved in an untoward manner. Maybe, who knows, he had all along been looking for an opportunity to go out and had seized that moment to do so. That is one of the tactics some men often employ against their spouses to get out of the house.

"Well, whatever it is, granted it is true, he has come by his wealth through the generosity of Alegeli, the rat. At least that is what he tells me. My question is, couldn't my husband ask for something better than wealth?" she mused. 'Here we are, married for fifteen years, with nothing to show for it. Not even a miscarriage to win the sympathy of my female colleagues and convince them that the fertility of my womb is not in doubt. Could my husband not have asked Alegeli to give him a child so that my compound, I mean our compound, too, might be filled with laughter and the cry of a baby like our neighbours'? Of what worth is wealth without a child? I need a baby I can rock in my arms and send to sleep with a lullaby...

Tuutuu... gbɔvi

Ttuutuu... gbɔvi.

Dada mele afea me o

Tata mele afea me o,

Ao dzedzevinye, bɔnu bɔnu kpoo!

But where do I find that child to enjoy my lullaby if my own husband won't give it to me? See how my babies' unrehearsed lullabies, strung like colourful beads are stuck deep in my throat, unsung, all because my husband has refused to offload the seeds in his groin into the fertile soil of my womb. Why wouldn't people say that you have sold your manhood to buy yourself wealth and self-importance that only fools admire?"

It had been questions heaped high upon questions now forming a mountain in a mind filled with utter despondency because there were no immediate answers, and there would not be any for a very long time to come. She remembered the lyrics of an old Agbadza song about the unpredictability of fate composed by Akpalu, the greatest composer and folklorist that ever lived in Ewe land. It was one of the songs most barren married women in the community often sang on days when their spirits were low:

"O Dzɔgbese!

O Dzɔgbese!

You have given me a raw deal.

Why have you lured me into this colourful trap?

You have succeeded in putting around this slim neck of mine,

This discoloured and faded Aggrey beads of a millstone

you call marriage.

The colour of my marriage, now an old dirty rag.

My shame is now a thing labeled " for sale" and tied high

up in the branches of the baobab tree at the market square.

The ladder to reach it and bring it down

Is locked up in my husband's groin

Or could it be in another man's room?

Or in another man's bed?

Tell me, Dzɔgbese!

Dzɔgbese, you have not been fair to me

Dzɔgbese you lied to me!

Dzɔgbese you cheated me! Dzɔgbese, you have betrayed

me!"

Picking the corner of her cover cloth, she wiped the steady
stream of tears flowing down her cheeks and gave a loud,
long mournful sigh, "Hmmmmm"

SECOND LEG

*Avɔfoditɔ medzuna ame o, adzaletɔe
dzuna ame.*

(The person whose cloth is dirty does
not insult others. It is rather the soap
seller who does.)

It had been two full moons after the last rains, marking the beginning of the special season when many things happened in the social life of the people of Sakabo. Nobody went to farm or hunting within the Sakabo community during this season. Forest animals had the freedom to breathe and breed without inhibition. With all the major work on the out farms done, people only looked forward to the harvest. Attention, more often, was on putting their houses, grain barns and other storage facilities in order in anticipation of an impending bumper harvest. It was a period for resting the body from the backbreaking job of tilling the land. This was also the period when most families spent more time on their backyard farms, closer to the homes and also mended their fences and repaired their roofs.

Children loved this season because they were spared those long daily treks to the outer farms that were located several kilometres away from home. According to Sakpli, it was also the period that most men had time to make their wives pregnant. No man worth his salt had any reason to deny his wife sex on the grounds of fatigue during this season. Any man who for reasons other than verifiable and certifiable ill-heath refused to satisfy his wife sexually during this season could be reported to the Sakabo Council of Elders by his wife for either non-performance, laziness in bed or denial of marital satisfaction. The punishment for such men could affect their sitting position in the general assembly of men subsequently. It was believed that any man who refused to sleep with his wife during this season was indirectly contributing towards the depopulation of Sakabo. Indeed, it was considered a crime against the spirit of multiplication that the Sakabo community was founded upon and therefore punished severely. The punishment could include demotion in rank, which was referred to as "shortening of the stem of one's tobacco pipe," especially where the culprit was a titled man. The other form of punishment was confinement of husband and wife in a room for a period not less than seven days, supervised by the Asafos. This was also the season when the Council of Elders sat to adjudicate matters of larceny, misdemeanor, infidelity and other crimes or social infractions committed within the community during the previous season.

Most of the issues the Council of Elders dealt with often fell into two categories. The first had to do with men and women who had been caught having sex on the bare earth on their farms. This act was considered a very serious taboo which required the culprits to undergo purification of themselves and the pacification of the spirit of the earth. It involved the slaughtering of a great number of sheep and fowls provided by the culprits. The second one involved persons who had been charged with harvesting game from other people's bush traps. There had been occasions when minors had been disciplined for stealing meat or fish from their mothers' cooking pots. It was indeed the season of justice. It was also the season when palm wine tappers made their money.

On one of the evenings during this season when the moon had adorned the tropical sky with her brightened fullness, a situation the children refer to as 'the season when the moon has had a thorough bath and smeared shea butter on its body,' the whole community came out to sit around huge bonfires to tell stories of the bravery of their ancestors. The bonfires were constantly stoked to spread the heat. From time to time, these fires would shoot wild tongues of giant reddish and sometimes yellowish flames, into the moonlit sky. Occasionally, some of the firewood would crack up and throw up sparkles of fireworks into the sky in a zigzag trajectory. The immediate surroundings around the adzido trees and the nearby bushes are intermittently illuminated, appearing as strange dancing silhouettes.

The women, after feeding their households and dealing with all the other essential chores, were free to join their men folk in the open, under the baobab trees, to watch their young children play under the moonlit sky. Sakabo tradition required that both sexes never mix on such occasions. The men always had to sit a little away from their women. Even among the men, there was still a way of separating the married ones from the bachelors. This was evident in the length of the stem of one's tobacco pipe. The longer the stem and the bigger the tobacco pot, the more responsible one was regarded in Sakabo. Here, responsibility and respect for a man was not premised on or solely defined by the size of a man's barn or kraal or the number of wives and children. It was a combination of all that but, above all, the length of the stem and the size of the pot of the man's tobacco pipe was a very important consideration. Legend had it that long ago, when Sakabo was very small community and even a toddler could crawl around it with ease, there lived a man called *Zadokeli.* He was considered the most prosperous and responsible person in the whole community. The stem and pot of his tobacco pipe was carried on the hefty shoulders of four strong young male children each time he came out to a public gathering. It was said that a puff on his pipe unleashed into the atmosphere billows of smoke equivalent to the amount of smoke produced when ten village huts were set ablaze.

However, Zadokeli died several years before the oldest person currently alive in Sakabo was born. Some say his grave was made extra long and extra deep to enable it accommodate his body and the object of his favourite pastime. Others also say it was rather his coffin, which was made of fired clay and shaped like a tobacco pipe. Both schools of thought agreed, however, that his tomb was filled with enough tobacco to last him another lifetime in the world of his ancestors.It came therefore as very little surprise to people from the nearby towns, even to this day, when young men in Sakabo found it fashionable to carry tobacco pipes whose stems did not only vary in size but were often exaggerated in length. In Sakabo, a man's greatest shame was to be referred to by another as *ezii-kpui*, a term that translates as "short-stem-piper." It was considered even more grievous and an unpardonable insult when it was uttered by a woman against a man because of the other obvious connotations it carried. Some men in Sakabo had been known to have committed suicide on account of such an insult from their women. Of course, other women had suffered severe battering and even multiple marital rape at the hands of their men for the same reason. 'Short-stem-piper' was therefore the most excruciating insult a woman could inflict on a man to arouse the beast in him. When uttered in public, it amounted to telling the man in the face and among his colleagues that he is lazy, useless and a good-for-nothing cockroach, both inside and outside the bedroom. Among the people of Sakabo therefore, *ezii-kpui* was a taboo word.

The young men in Sakabo struggled to outdo each other in hard work and entrepreneurship. Those who took to fishing made sure they were the best in their profession and so did the food crop farmers, wood carvers, weavers, ironmongers, and traders in salt. Laziness had no place in the community.

Even though all the men were grouped together smoking their clay pipes of various shapes and sizes, they still had a sitting arrangement so subtly structured that separated the men from the boys, distinguishing achievers from non-achievers. There had been a few occasions when a relatively younger person, in terms of age, had joined the senior ranks of achievers. This was usually by dint of some exceptional heroic exploits by the young fellow in the service of the community. According to Sakabo tradition, when a housefly performs a great feat, it ceases to be a common housefly and instead is referred to as *togbato* or tsetsefly.

On such evenings, as decreed by custom, Sakabo women would sit a bit far away from their men, often under another adzido tree, which was usually smaller in size than that of their husbands and quite close to their children who played nearby. This way, the mothers were able to keep their eyes on their children who played together to ensure that their freedom under the moonlit sky was not unduly misused or abused, and still be able to eavesdrop on their husbands' conversation.

There had been occasions in the past when boys had tried to take undue advantage of their female playmates. However, the vigilance of the mothers had always ensured a timely rescue of the little girls before their male playmates could attempt any naughtiness. The sanctions prescribed by the elders whenever such unfortunate juvenile excesses occurred were so swift and severe that no child ever dreamt of misbehaving during playtime on moonlit nights in Sakabo. The last time such a thing occurred in Sakabo, as far as living memory could recollect, the community set ablaze the houses of the parents of the offending male child and banished them from the community. The rule, however, was that they could only return to Sakabo when everyone who knew about the incident that led to their being exiled within the community had died. Of course, they knew it was a euphemistic way of saying the family had been banished in perpetuity.

The children often confined their games to the sunset-end of the small *adzido* tree under which the mothers, by custom, had comfortably created their colony. This way, the mothers became a buffer between the playing children and the fathers at the far end. This arrangement also ensured that the children never crossed over to interrupt the business of their fathers and uncles.

Often times, young children, numbering about fifteen and between the ages of ten and sixteen, formed a circle to play the game of Tingoro-Ta. The origin of this children's game was steeped in obscurity. What most people said was that the game was as old as the village. Others said it was older than the village. The elderly people in the village had a contrary opinion, which they often expressed proverbially thus, 'The beard is never older than the eye brow'. The village drunkard, Sakpli, as one would expect, always had his own more picturesque response on the issue and this seemed to have gained more appreciation among the youth. He was fond of saying "The palm wine can never be taller than the calabash in which it is fetched". When asked to explain further what he meant by that, he said, "The town of Sakabo is the calabash and the story is trapped within the calabash like the frothy palm wine. The independence and the territorial integrity of the palm wine is meaningless unless it allows itself to be confined within the physical periphery defined by the calabash. The palm wine can never have an independent existence. The calabash owns the palm wine and not the other way round. I, Sakpli, say so. If you want to hear more from me on this interesting subject, get me a calabash of palm wine and I shall give you a practical demonstration of what I am saying."

This way, Sakpli managed to get willing people to offer him free palm wine to drink. No wonder he was always drunk. According to sources, the only time he was sober was when he felt the pains and pangs of hunger.

To start the game of *Tingoro-ta*, the entire children bunched up together holding hands with eyes tightly shut and going round the wooden 'pole of honour' planted firmly in the centre. One of the elderly women would step out from her group with a rag in hand and walk towards the children. When she got close to them, she threw the rag into the sky and while it was still airborne, she shouted "*Nade tso dzi gbɔna looo!*" This was the signal to the children to open their eyes and run for cover from a strange 'object' falling from the sky. The unfortunate child on whose head or body the rag fell automatically became the centre person who would stand by the 'pole of honour' at the centre to call out the twenty Tingoro-ta questions.

In a situation where the 'rag of dishonor' touched nobody, the children quickly rallied round again in their circle and the elderly woman went through the process again till a victim was found and brought to the centre of the circle next to the pole. As his peers blindfolded the child with the 'rag of dishonour', the rest formed a circle around him, facing outwards. Upon each question from their blindfolded colleague, those forming the circle took two steps forward in any direction of their choice whilst answering the question. Whoever answered the twentieth question or was successfully sought after and touched with the 'rag of dishonour' after the last question had been asked assumed the centre position and became the new bearer of 'the rag of dishonour.' The interesting thing, however, was that even though the questions were fixed in a particular order, the centre-person had the creative liberty to outwit his colleagues by randomly shuffling the position of the last question, thereby catching any inattentive participant off-guard.

"Nuka goro!?" he would say at the top of his voice for the mothers sitting under their tree to hear.

"Goro fa nya!" A resounding response from his colleagues would cut through the evening quietness, as they took their first two steps away from the person at the center.

Nuka Fa nya?

Fanya Doko!

Nuka Doko?

Doko Gbiya!

Nuka Gbiya?

Gbiya Segede!

Nuka Segede?

Segede Gboo!

Nuka Gboo?

Efo Kodjo Mawugbe

Gboo kple Atsi!
Nuka Tsi?
Tsi Dzaa!
Nuka Dzaa?
Dzaa Luu!
Nuka Luu?
Luu Xee!
Nuka Xee?
Xee Gbɔgbɔe!
Nuka Gbɔgbɔe?
Gbɔgbɔe Mi da!
Nukae Mi da...?

This would be the centre-person's last question, expecting some one not concentrating enough to answer and thereby trade places with him. *Nukae Mi da...?* More often than not this last question, which was considered the trap, had always been left hanging in the air unanswered. For as long as it so remained, the centre-person would keep repeating it as he went about seeking the rest of the group who by now would have all gone into hiding. The idea was for the centre-person to track a respondent and touch him or her with the 'rag of dishonour' before the respondent touched base at the pole in the centre of the circle. Whilst the seeker left the base at the centre going to track those in hiding, the rest also tried to sneak back into the centre of the circle. Each person that touched base shouted the answer to the last question "Mi

23

da Tingoro Ta!" The centre-person as the seeker was not expected to move too far away from the centre pole which would be the touch-base for his returning colleagues. His aim was to touch any part of their bodies with the rag of dishonour before they touched the centre pole. That was the only way he could redeem himself and get someone else to take over from him. The game continued until the mothers thought and felt their children had had enough. They would then call the game off and send the children home to bed. There had been occasions when someone had played the centre-person all through the night because he had been unable to find anyone to transfer the task of centre-person to.

The story was told of Fafali who when she had to play the centre-person one night cleverly outwitted her colleagues by placing a scare-crow she had made with some old rags and sticks from her mother's kitchen at the centre of the circle before going to look for her friends in hiding. It did not take her too long to flush them out of their hideouts and get someone to take over from her.

The very first boy to run out of his hideout got so scared upon seeing the effigy that he could not approach the centre of the circle. He was simply scared stiff and started screaming for his mother. Fafali, who had been hiding nearby, just stepped out and coolly laid the rag of dishonour on the head of the

screaming colleague. It was a story told with great relish by children in Sakabo even to this day.

There were days when the weather did not permit the children to play outdoors. On such occasions, the most elderly woman in the community took it upon herself to gather the children around in one of the houses to tell them riddles or folktales as passed on to her by her own grandmother. Storytelling among the people of Sakabo was considered serious business. It formed an integral part of the informal educational system that ensured the requisite indigenous wisdom, knowledge and skills were transferred from one generation to the next without a hitch. A popular folktale that almost every child above the age of ten knew how to tell had to do with a wicked King by name Adzida. This particular story had gained much currency because it was told by every old lady at the least opportunity. Like all folktales, it began with *"Mise egli loo!"* and the children responded with one loud excited voice *"Egli ne va!"*

"Once upon a time..." the story went, "...there lived an old lady by name Mama Zigi and Emefa, her pretty eighteen year old grand daughter in a cottage in the forest on the outskirts of Abo where King Adzida was the ruler. One early morning, the chief gong-gong beater of the overlord of Abo announced that the king was inviting all maidens above the age of eighteen who had undergone puberty rites to the palace. The purpose of the invitation was to enable the prince to choose one of the maidens for a wife. On hearing this news, Emefa pleaded with her grandmother to allow her to visit the palace, but Mama Zigi would have nothing to do with the palace of King Adzida. However, Emefa pressed her grandmother to allow how to go and try her luck. Maybe, who knew, the prince might select her and that would mean a change in their fortunes. Mama Zigi finally yielded, reluctantly though, to Emefa's persistent pleas to be allowed to attend the function. She dressed her up in the best silk and *ago* cloth she had kept in her wardrobe. She brought out her expensive, colourful, Krobo royal beads to adorn her neck. Then, she said to Emefa, "Now, you can go."

But Emefa had another request. "Grandma, I want you to go with me to the palace"

"Not me. I can't go there," the old woman replied with such bluntness that left Emefa a bit bemused.

"Why, Grandma?" asked Emefa. For an answer Mama Zigi sang a song:

"Vɔnu ti a dome,

Nye ma yi vɔnu ti a do me o Vɔnu ti a dome

Nye ma yi vɔnu ti a dome Vɔnu ti a dome

Nye ma yi vɔnu ti a dome o Funyetɔ wo ta ne me yi tɔ nye
ma dzɔ

Funye tɔ wo taa ne meyi tɔ nye ma dzɔ Funye tɔ wo taa ne
meyi tɔ nye ma dzɔ!"

'Grandma, there is more to this song than meets the ear. There seems to be something you are hiding from me. Please, Grandma, why are you saying the palace is like a trial court and your innocence can not be guaranteed? Again, who are these enemies for which reason you do not want to approach the palace of Adzida?

26

'Do you really want to know the story?'

'Yes, Grandma.'

'You may not like the ending, so do not let me begin to tell it.'

'Grandma, don't forget I am over eighteen years old and have undergone confinement that transforms girls into women.'

'Well, if you say so. Since you insist, I shall tell you the whole truth and nothing but the truth. Pull that stool over here and sit.' Emefa obeyed.

Mama Zigi began:

"Many years ago, long before you were born, the same King, Adzida, summoned all women above the age of sixty to his palace and accused them of being witches and instantly exiled them from his kingdom. Those women who tried to resist lost their lives in very outrageous and mysterious circumstances that cannot be easily recounted.

As if that was not enough, years later Adzida issued another decree which made it a crime for women to give birth to baby girls. Any pregnant woman who gave birth to a baby girl surrendered the baby to the palace executioners who took care of the baby in a nice way."

'Mama, were the executioners nursing mothers?' Asked Emefa.

'The executioners were ordered to kill the babies' Mama Zigi said in a low whisper to her granddaughter.

'Oh no!' exclaimed Emefa, as she covered her mouth with her hand in utter disbelief.

"Well, as fate would have it, it turned out that one of the King's wives was pregnant at the time this decree came into effect. When her time was due, she gave birth to a baby girl but instead of handing the baby over to the executioners, she woke up at dawn and went into the forest where she abandoned the day-old baby near an anthill and told anyone who cared to know that she had had a miscarriage. That morning, one of the old women who had been declared a witch and had relocated to a lonely cottage on the outskirts of the forest, was on her way to the farm when she heard the wailing of a baby in the forest. It was obvious to her from the manner the baby was crying that it was in distress. Could it be that the mother of the baby was in some form of trouble and could not attend to the baby… or it was a stolen baby? As the thoughts floated through her mind, she cautiously made her way through the thick, thorny undergrowth towards the thicket where the baby's cry was coming from. Finally, she got to the anthill and there was the poor day-old baby with its umbilical cord still intact wrapped up in plantain leaves with the deadly red ants called alilɔ swarming all over it. Some of the ants had found their way into the baby's eyes, nostrils, mouth and ears. The baby was in real torment. The old woman quickly rescued the poor baby girl and brushed the tormenting ants from her body. At a point, she had to put her mouth to the nostrils and ears of the baby to suck out the obstinate ants that had stuck in there. The old woman did not continue to her farm that day. Instead, she went back to her cottage with the baby and after cleaning her up smeared her body with palm oil to soothe her pains from the poisonous stings of the red ants.

Since she had no breast milk to feed the baby, she arranged with a palm wine tapper in the next village to supply her on a daily basis with the fresh, very milky sweet first sap. It was this stuff that the old woman fed the baby with until she was ready to take in solid food".

'So, the baby survived'

'Of course, she did survive. She is now a pretty nineteen year old girl'

'Grandma, can you show me where she lives?'

'Why?'

'I wish to be her friend'

'Go get me a mirror from the room' Emefa hurried into the room and came out with the mirror

'Here you are Grandma, the mirror.'

'Look into the mirror.' Emefa obeyed.

'Whose face do you see staring at you in there?'

'I see my own face.'

'That's it.'

'That's it… What is it…?'

"No sooner had the question dropped from her lips than the answer hit her like a huge thunderbolt."

'Grandma…Do you mean I am that … And you are the old woman in your story?'

'Yes, my child, now you know the truth about yourself.'

"Emefa stepped forward to sweep Mama Zigi in a powerful embrace."

'Oh Grandma, thank you for saving my life. I shall never leave you, Grandma,' said Emefa, as she dried the tears on her face with the back of her hand.

'Well, now you know the truth, and it means you can't marry the prince. He is your brother.' '
That is so, but I would like to meet my father, if you don't mind.'
'That's a very tough request but I'll see what I can do. I don't think there is any use stopping you now.'
'Thank you, Grandma.'
'However, my status as an outcast will not allow me to enter Adzidakɔfe with you. I shall wait for you at the crossroads where the footpath to Sakpanu meets the one from Zegle.'
'But Grandma, how would he know that I am his daughter?' asked Emefa.
"Mama Zigi told her not to worry. She made Emefa sit next to her and she taught her a song she should sing as soon as she stepped into the courtyard of the palace:

Tɔnye Adzida deee Tɔnye Adzida deee

Ewoe wɔ nu be ela wo ne du maaee... Tɔnye Adzida deee

Tɔnye Adzida deee

Ewoe wɔ nu be ela wo ne du maaee Alea wo le atsu ne ne

nɔe ne ne Aleke a wo lea atsu ne ne nɔe ne ne Miawoe nye

tɔnu fevia wo

Adzida dzi nyɔnuvi a

Adzida koe de alilɔ wo do mee

Trɔsiviwoe menyo nam o

Ne me nyo alilɔ woe la du ma ee

Avalu sia woeeee

30

Efo Kodjo Mawugbe

Woe nya wli na do eeeee

Indeed, when Emefa finally stepped into the courtyard of the palace her outfit, particularly the expensive Krobo beads on her neck and ankles, made everyone look in her direction. When she eventually allowed the song to be carried gently aloft by her melodious voice, the whole palace went quiet. She sang it through one more time.

By this time, the attentive ears of the audience, including King Adzida and his wife, had picked up the lyrics. They understood the fact that she was of royal blood, a true princess abandoned at the mercy of red *alilɔ* ants and would have died but for the compassion of another human being who came to her rescue. As Emefa kept on singing, the King could no longer remain on his throne. He stood up from his throne on the dais and with slow, deliberate steps made his way towards Emefa, followed by his wife. When he got closer he threw his arms wide open and said to Emefa 'Indeed I am your father and you are my daughter. Come into my arms' the king embraced Emefa and from that day she became part of the royal family at the palace. Emefa succeeded in convincing her father to repeal the two obnoxious laws that declared women above the age of sixty witches and had them outlawed and the other one that criminalised the birth of baby girls. Emefa brought into the palace a new breeze and a fresh breath of life and joy that was to sweep through every home in Adzidakɔfe and beyond. And they all lived happily thereafter."

Quite often, long after the story was over, the children would be heard singing the songs in the folktale and this was always perceived by the elders as a strong indication that they did not only enjoy the story but could be relied upon as conduits for its transmission to the next generation. It was said in Sakabo that a good folktale was like cured tobacco - only the gum of old people can attest to its potency.

THIRD LEG

Hia metua ame wodoa afɔ tonu o.

(When you are miserable, you do not support your chin with your feet.)

A t the palace, Torgbuiga Ashi Aklama II, the chief of Sakabo and his elders had just finished trying a case involving Azalo, one of the notorious young men in the village. Daavi, the *akpeteshie* and palm wine seller, had dragged the young man to the palace accusing him of having stolen her pregnant goat. During the trial, it was proven that the goat found in Azalo's possession indeed belonged to Daavi. However, Azalo insisted he did not steal the goat.

Asked to explain how the goat came to be tethered to a pole in his compound, Azalo had this to say: "Daavi needed someone to do a painting job for her. I offered to do it. According to the terms mutually arrived at, she was to give me half of the total amount charged in advance to enable me mobilise the necessary logistics for the job. She was to make full payment after certifying that the job was satisfactorily done. I got a few friends together and we managed to finish the job in record time. When I went to her to collect the rest of the money due me, she began to give excuses."

"What kind of excuses?" asked one of the elders.

"According to her, she was expecting me to take three weeks to complete the job but my colleagues and I did it in three days, so she was going to give me only three days' wages."

"Hold it there", interjected Amenke Kini, popularly nicknamed Amega Gaxa, a strong-willed, white-bearded octogenarian. His nickname *'Gaxa'* was a direct reference to his untrimmed moustache, which most people said resembled an iron broom. He hardly spoke during arbitrations. His voice therefore commanded attention anytime he spoke. When he was certain he had arrested everyone's attention, he slowly panned his gaze to take in Daavi at the far end of the horse-shoe sitting arrangement where she sat in between the two daughters she had brought as witnesses.

"Daavi"

"Amega, I am all ears".

"Is it true what the young man here says?" he asked in his aged but firm voice.

"It is so, my elder".

"Now, tell me this, did your agreement with the young man stipulate he was going to be paid on a daily basis or after he had completed the entire job to your satisfaction?"

There was a long pause as Daavi and her daughters conferred in whispers to determine the best response to give Amega Gaxa. The question hung in the silence like an over-ripe fruit about to drop from a tree.

"Well...errmm... you see... errrm... he made me to... errmm... understand the job was going to take... errmm... three weeks and... we agreed on a price. But he... did it in just three days and... I felt he had cheated me", Daavi stuttered.

"Weren't you satisfied with the job the young man and his friends did?" Amega Gaxa asked.

"I was," Daavi answered.

"In what way then do you say this young man here cheated you? The elders seated here would like to know" Amega Gaxa demanded.

35

There was a hectic conference between the two sisters and heir mother as they all seemed to be in disagreement about something. The answer to Amega Gaxa's question was not forthcoming. Azalo was politely asked to continue with his disputation. Emboldened by this initial setback encountered by his accusers in their submission courtesy the grey-bearded octogenarian, Azalo narrated to Torgbuiga and his elders how the plaintiff breached their contract with impunity.

"According to her, the workers who had come to help me execute the job drank her local gin on credit to the tune of an amount equal to the rest of the money she was to give me. By her calculations therefore, everything squared up. She owed me nothing and I also owed her nothing." Almost everyone was reeling with laughter by the time Azalo finished his statement.

When the question was put to Daavi as to the veracity of Azalo's statement, she said it was so and her daughters confirmed selling liquor to Azalo's friends. Asked whether he was aware his workers drank liquor on credit, Azalo said he knew, but he was in no way privy to the payment terms agreed upon by Daavi and her customers. Daavi herself did not deny this assertion by Azalo. On the substantial issue of the stolen pregnant goat, Azalo submitted he had been to Daavi's house that day to demand his outstanding debt.

Before he set off, he made sure he had taken in some *sodabi* to embolden him to stand up like a man and deal with Daavi and her two daughters once and for all. On arrival at Daavi's house, he learnt she had gone out. However, the behaviour of her two daughters made him suspect that Daavi might be hiding in the room. So, he decided to take a seat and wait for her. This did not go down well with the two daughters who insisted he leave their premises or go and wait outside the house and not at the joint where he would be a nuisance to customers.

Initially, Azalo refused to budge but upon second thought, decided to comply. He waited for more than eight hours outside Daavi's house. He had obviously become tired and was about to abandon his mission and leave for home when he stumbled upon a piece of rope lying on the ground that he thought could make a clothes line. He picked up the rope and dragged it along all the way home. On reaching home, he was so drunk that he could not remember what he actually did with the rope. When it was put to him he tied the end of the rope to a pole in his house, he said, "If that pole is meant for a drying line then it is highly possible." He swore by the breasts of the goddess of River Gbaga, that he did not realise there was a pregnant goat at the other end of the rope. He maintained that as far as his drunken memory could recollect, it was only a piece of loose rope he had picked from the ground. Some of the elders found his story quite amusing but most unlikely, whilst others thought otherwise. "Judging by the stubborn character of goats that we all know, it is most unlikely anybody could drag a goat through the village in broad day light without attracting attention.

The animal would definitely give one away by bleating loudly", One of the elders sitting across from Amega Gaxa proffered. Of course, everyone knew that sheep were docile to the point of stupidity but the same could not be said of goats. Goats seldom surrendered easily to capture. This view was premised on a local anecdote that every child in Sakabo was familiar with. It was said that one day Goat and Sheep were journeying back home on a passenger truck from a far away village where they had attended a mutual friend's funeral. On reaching their destination Goat, who had no money in his pocket because he had used his last coin to buy alcohol to entertain his friends at the funeral, decided to bolt away as soon as the speeding vehicle screeched to a stop. Sheep, who did not know why his friend had taken to his heels walked confidently to the driver to pay his fare.

On giving the money to the driver, he was expecting the driver to give him change. The driver decided to deduct the fare of Goat from the money paid to him by Sheep. Sheep's protestations intended to make the driver rescind his decision obviously fell on deaf ears. The driver went ahead and deducted Goat's transport fare from the money given to him by Sheep and drove off. This action of the driver infuriated Sheep so much that he swore that any time or anywhere he met the driver he was going to demand his change. Goat, on the other hand, adopted a more cautious and survivalist approach that made him avoid vehicles and their drivers wherever and whenever the two came face to face. This accounts for why between goats and sheep, the latter easily is killed at random by motor vehicles.

"It is possible he may have offered the goat a kingly ride on his shoulders all the way to his house," someone tossed in. "If it were a sheep, that's acceptable but not a goat. Unless, may be, in this particular case, there was a reversal of roles and it was the goat that rather carried Azalo to his house", Gaxa chipped in, obviously as comic relief. Soon, it was time for Torgbuiga's Tsami, the spokesperson, to deliver the verdict of the court of Elders after they had excused themselves for a few minutes and gone into kpɔvi- conclave, to arrive at an acceptable and amicable consensus. He stepped forward, cleared his throat and called for attention.

"Ago-o-o-o!"

"Ame-e-e-!" the gathering responded.

"Having offered fair hearing to both the accused and the accuser, I am here to present the verdict arrived at the conclave of Torgbuiga and his elders", he paused briefly. "On the substantial issue of how Daavi's pregnant goat mysteriously travelled from Dzigbe to the Anyigbe quarter of the town without detection, Torgbuiga and his elders think the matter needs to be thoroughly investigated. We are equally aware that the goat in question is alive. Even as I speak to you now, the pregnant goat has been granted asylum in Torgbuiga's palace where it shall remain as a four-legged living exhibit until we of the palace have been able to demystify the circumstances surrounding its migration from one end of town to the other in broad day light, without detection".

"Torgbuiga and his elders further established the fact that Daavi indeed did employ the services of Azalo and has not fulfilled the terms of their mutual agreement as far as remuneration goes. It is the considered view of Torgbuiga and his elders that Daavi honour fully the terms of the contract she has with Azalo by paying him in full the remainder of his money as stipulated in their agreement. It is also the considered view of Torgbuiga and his elders that Azalo cannot be held culpable for the debt owed by his friends to Daavi. She is therefore not justified in deducting that debt from the money she owes Azalo. Torgbuiga and his elders are however ever ready to sit and listen to Daavi, if and whenever she is willing to initiate charges against those three young men who drank without payment. This is the voice of Torgbuiga and his distinguished elders. My lips have come together."

The full import of the goat being "palace exhibit" was not in any way lost on the members of Torgbuiga's arbitration committee. The truth was that that was the fee Daavi was indirectly paying for bringing a case before the adjudicating Council of Elders of Sakabo. At an appointed date and time, these elders would assemble at the palace for a meal of goat pepper-soup, served with yam fufu and that would be the funeral of the four-legged living exhibit. Nobody questioned Sakabo justice. You would be told in clear court language that that it was the custom. Whenever gifts found their way into a palace, they never found their way back. That was the custom. What one might however wish to know was, since when did the goat in question become a gift presented to the palace?

One could read the pain and disappointment etched across the contortions on the faces of Daavi and her daughters.

Even though it was obvious she had been offered a raw deal, she could not complain or lodge an appeal. Since time immemorial, nobody had won a case on appeal in the traditional court of justice at Sakabo. As a daughter of the community, she knew once the Council of Elders had spoken she had no option but to comply, no matter how bitter she might be feeling. Slowly, she unfastened the knot in the corner of her cloth and counted some mutilated notes and coins which she handed to the daughter next to her, who passed it on to the elder closest to her, who in turn relayed it to another elder till it finally arrived in the safe hands of Tsami who counted it again. Tsami openly announced the total amount in his hands to the gathering. He then whispered something to Torgbuiga and then called Azalo and handed the money to him, amidst a triumphant shout from a handful few of the young people that had gathered in the palace to listen to the verdict. For these young men, Azalo's victory was theirs as well.

It was, as they were wont to claim, a sweet victory by one of their own over a perceived enemy who sought to make drunkards of the young men in Sakabo. No sooner had Togbuiga declared the sitting over than the young men rushed forward to sweep Azalo off his feet. They carried him

shoulder high out of the palace into the narrow streets of
Sakabo, where the jubilation continued. Nobody took notice
of Daavi or her two daughters any longer. The arbitration
was over. The accuser and accused had all gone home. Some
twisted form of justice had been dispensed. Nobody appeared
to see the crooked path of justice in Sakabo. It was time to
drink fresh palm wine and muse over other trifles. Tɔgbuiga
and his elders were still sitting, informally though, trying
to relive some of the hilarious moments of the submissions
made during the just-ended trial. It was no secret that it was
during these informal sessions that the date for the slaughter
of the quadruped was decided, even as they quaffed the fresh
palm wine, Incidentally, on this occasion before that decision
on the animal could be taken, someone announced himself
at the gates of the inner courtyard of the palace with a very
loud *"Ago-o-o-o!"*

Momentarily, all activities ceased and all heads turned
towards the direction of the palace entrance. "Let goodness
enter our abode and let evil remain behind" Tsami Atsuga
responded.

It took quite a while before the left side of the double leafed
palace gate swung open very slowly. First, it was a dry left
foot in a worn out and over-used sandals made from raw hide
but now held together by a piece of forest twine and made
dirty by many weeks of accumulated dust that appeared. The
dark heel of the dirty foot was cracked in several parts by the
unrepentant harmattan, creating a design of creeks of caked

dust forming little dried river beds running down to the sole.

Just when the foot was firmly planted over the threshold, a hand followed. This was a blister-thickened palm with dry knotty fingers of a person who might have had a bit of crocodile skin wrapped over his hands. The gate swung three-quarters open to reveal the stomach, wrapped up in a faded shirt that hung loosely above the navel, woefully failing to conceal it. The gate finally swung fully open. He stepped into the palace courtyard, tugged on his shirt as if by some miracle he could add a few more inches to its length to enable it cover his bloated calabash-like stomach that carried his large protruding navel.

"Aaaah, so it is you, Sakpli," the assembly muttered, barely concealing the revulsion they had for him.

"Yeah, man, it is me!" he responded with great self-satisfaction as he thumped his chest with pride. Approaching them, he declared, "I am the only living legend whose ears are able to pick information from under water, under the earth and over the clouds. Even those that are spoken between a husband and wife under the sheets, behind closed doors, filter into my ears."

"Sakpli eto lakpa!" someone shouted.

"Sakpli eto gobo!" another elder called out, all in apparent reference to the size of Sakpli's ears which everyone, including Sakpli, agreed were unusually large for one person. However, Sakpli was not a man to take offence at such derogative remarks. As he often said with great aplomb, "It is not as if I bought the pair of ears from the market or went and borrowed them from Mawu Sogbo Lisa's warehouse. It is the creator God Himself, who in His infinite wisdom gave them to me, Sakpli, at the point of creation for a purpose." His personal philosophy had always been that a real man was the one that possessed and demonstrated the capacity to turn negative circumstances and even vile comments about himself into great opportunities. To such a person, every insult was a window of opportunity to assess himself and the person who uttered the insult. "Yes, that's me. The monkey says his eyes are his oracle. The monkey lives by the principle of 'seeing-is believing' but I say my ears are my oracle. It is what enters my ears that I believe and not what I see." By such statements, Sakpli was able to get everyone reeling in rib-splitting laughter. Sakpli did not allow anyone to offer him a seat. He dragged one nearby that had been vacated by the plaintiffs in the just-ended arbitration and made himself comfortable. "Yes, I am now properly seated", he said, as he looked at the almost-overflowing pot of frothy palm wine with the corner of his eyes and licked his lips. No one remembered that Sakpli had not formally greeted the gathering, as custom demanded, before taking his seat.

"So, you are now seated, what next?" Amega Gaxa asked. "What next is that which placidly lies inside that pot. I mean the frothy stuff you people have been sending down your throats all day. Pass me the calabash and let me also wet my parched throat," he demanded, snatching an empty calabash from one of the elders next to him and ordering the server to fill it to the brim.

"Sakpli eto ga!" an elder bellowed.

"Yes, that is me. It is even said that after molding my ears, Dzɔgbese Lisa did not have enough clay left to carry on with other people's ears. That is what accounts for people like you and you and you having smaller, mouse-like ears as compared to mine,"he added, pointing in the direction of a few of the elders with his right forefinger. This drew loud laughter from the elders. Sakpli quickly drank his first calabash of the fresh palm wine and asked for a second helping. He kept them rocking with so much laughter with his witticism and wisecracks that they could not even find the strength to continue drinking. Sakpli took advantage of this and helped himself to calabashful after calabashful of the frothy palmwine. It was little wonder then that by midday, when most of the elders were ready to depart, Sakpli was sitting on the floor leaning against one of the pillars, not only asleep but snoring loudly with saliva trickling down from the corner of his mouth on to his chest and crawling towards his navel. Torgbuiga asked that Sakpli be left alone. He further instructed Apedomeshie, his eldest wife, to prepare some food for Sakpli when he finally came round.

FOURTH LEG

Fia de se medea nukoko se o.

(A chief makes all laws but not
laws against laughter.)

Efo Kodjo Mawugbe

Only very few people still living in Sakabo knew Sakpli very well. He used to be a village teacher-cum-letter writer-cum-foreign language interpreter in Akpadikɔfe, a farming and fishing community with a sizeable population several kilometres away on the other side of the Gbaga River beyond Tɔgodo. He was semi-literate but could fairly read and write the language of the Whiteman. The early European traders who came to sell their wares on the coast and the missionaries, who were desirous of spreading the gospel into the interior as part of their civilising mission mandate, found him an indispensable ally. The two groups at some point in time fought over him and often showered gifts on him as a way of wooing him to their side.

Sakpli's popularity as the only indigene in the whole area who could understand and communicate in the Whiteman's language was quite legendary. All the important visitors who paid courtesy calls on his chief had to, as a sign of respect, also pay him a visit to acknowledge his role as the sole interpreter of the Whiteman's language. Sakpli, more or less, became the unofficial chief of Akpadikɔfe, his hometown, in the eyes of some people.

Some even said he was becoming more popular than his chief and found a way of warning the latter to be wary of his official interpreter. The chief was advised to take steps to clip

47

Sakpli's wings lest he usurped his position. Thus the seeds of discord, unjustified hatred and jealousy were carefully sown in the heart of the Chief against one of his industrious subjects. Incidentally, within the same palace, there were those who were secretly symapathetic towards Sakpli and therefore did not hesitate to leak back to him the diabolical machinations of the Chief to eliminate him because he was perceived as a threat to the stool. When he was first hinted about the Chief's dangerous plot, Sakpli took it for a joke and dismissed it with the contempt he thought it deserved.

Then strange things began to happen that initially he thought were just mere coincidences. Upon sober reflection, however, he was convinced they were orchestrations by the hands and minds of evil men living within his own community. First, it was his thirty-acre maize farm inter-cropped with cassava which was ravaged by bushfire under very mysterious circumstances when the crops were almost ready for harvest. The tubers of cassava were left roasted and wasted in the bowels of the scorched earth. As if that was not painful enough, two of his fishing canoes capsized with his fishing gear on river Gbaga in broad day light. Not too long after that, thieves raided his home to steal the new fishing gear he had purchased to replace the lost one and vandalised other property he had taken years to acquire.

In all these cases, he made reports at the palace, but no action was taken. The perpetrators of those reprehensible acts were never found, let alone apprehended. It did not take him too long to figure out the long hand of Akpadikɔfe royal house in these personal setbacks. Sakpli decided to do the one thing that he thought was noble and honourable under the circumstances, and this meant severing all personal and diplomatic ties with the royal house of Akpadikɔfe to safeguard his life. It was an act of self-preservation and survival in the midst of relatives and close pals who had suddenly become enemies. He stopped visiting the palace and would no longer serve as its official interpreter during visits by foreign dignitaries. Instead, he sought to drown his sorrows in alcohol. It was this act of seeking refuge in alcohol, more than any other, that would lead the once brilliant interpreter on the path of self-destruction from which he would never recover. What finally sent him packing baggage and all and fleeing Akpadikɔfe by night was the insulting message the chief sent to him regarding an expedition the elders in the palace thought should have Sakpli as Team Leader. This was a few years after the multiple disasters had struck his farm and fishing boats and had caused him to take to excessive drinking.

The issue had to do with a young girl by name Maria Amedzro, the daughter of the catechist of the Presbyterian Church at Yesukpodzi, the Christian quarter of Akpadikɔfe. Originally, Yesukpodzi began as a small settlement carved out of Akpadikɔfe by the Christian missionaries to separate, protect and insulate the local converts from their idol worshipping, non-Christian kith and kin. Many citizens of Akpadikɔfe and the surrounding villages who by their utterances, deeds, omission or commission fell foul to the customs and traditions of their people escaped customary justice by seeking refuge in Yesukpodzi. There, they were made to renounce their traditional past, confess the Lord Jesus as their personal saviour, and get baptised. They were given Biblical names, mostly from the Old Testament, such as Obadiah, Jehu, Zimri, Jezebel and became Christians who were offered full citizenship of the Yesukpodzi community. By this act these fugitives, now born-again Christians, no longer felt bound or governed by the customary laws of Akpadikɔfe. The often-quoted scripture to stress and support this contentious position was to be found in the eighth chapter of the book of Romans, where it is stated; "There is therefore NOW no condemnation to them which are in Christ Jesus who walk not after the flesh but after the spirit."

At a point in time when the population of the new settlement had increased tremendously, the elders of the Christian settlement attempted to change the name to *Akpadikɔfe* Number Two. The Chief and his people vehemently resisted this attempt. According to the chief, from the days of yore there had always been one Akpadikɔfe and so would it remain.

The Chief swore an oath on the graves of his departed fathers that he would resist with his very last breath any attempt to make him go down in history as the one who superintended the disintegration of the unitary state bequeathed him. The mere thought of Yesukpodzi subtly seeking a new, equal and independent status as Akpadikɔfe Number Two, according to Sakpli, could be likened to the anthill asking the land on which it rested to shift so the anthill could increase its size. In order to make sure that those living in the Christian settlement recognised the authority of the overlord of an undivided Akpadikɔfe on whose land their church stood, the elders of Akpadikɔfe conspired to teach the Christian settlers a lesson.

On a very cold rainy night when the Christians were asleep the Asafo, made up of the youth of Akpadikɔfe under the command of Sakpli, swiftly moved stealthily into Yesukpodzi and made away with the huge brass church bell that hung high up a wooden tower which was used in summoning converts to worship every dawn. On this particular dawn and for the first time ever, the bell did not toll in Yesukpodzi. The Christians overslept. The message was clear, and the lesson was well learnt. The ambitious and impudent secession was quickly nipped in the bud.

Yesukpodzi humbled itself before Akpadikɔfe. The captured church bell remained in the house of Sakpli as war booty to commemorate what became known in the history of Akpadikɔfe as the Gamadigbe campaign. This gave birth to the annual Gamadigbeza Festival, celebrated by the chiefs and people of Akpadikɔfe not only to commemorate the daring bravery of the Asafo company, but more importantly, to reinforce the fact that Yesukpodzi and her numerous Christian converts and future believers, shall forever remain a vassal settlement of Akpadikɔfe.

It was from this Christian community that Maria Amedzro, the seventeen-year-old daughter of Zacheus Amedzro, the resident catechist, was tried by the council of elders of the church for fornication, adultery and getting pregnant out of acceptable wedlock. This was a law the Catechist had impressed upon the church elders to adopt some eighteen years earlier when his daughter was only a six-month-old foetus in his wife's womb. He believed it was the right code of ethics designed, in accordance with Biblical principles, to guide the youth within the church on to the path of righteousness and high morality. Little did it occur to Zacheus then that someday he would be asked to supervise and administer the bitter pill he had painfully offered many a wayward young boy and girl to his own daughter.

It did not require a gynecologist to prove that Maria, the Catechist's daughter, was pregnant. According to Sister Abigail, the only woman on the council, the symptoms were overwhelming. "Maria's ankles are swollen, her palms are white, and the eyes have receded a bit into their sockets. She has been spitting about incessantly and above all, her stomach is bulging which cannot, under any circumstance, be attributed to overfeeding since there is severe drought and famine this year. For me, Maria is fully pregnant."

The elders, after listening to Sister Abigail's submission, quickly retired into kpɔvi, to confer and arrive at a unanimous verdict. All this while, Maria sat quietly on a small kitchen stool kept in the far away corner of the chapel for people accused of committing that type of crime. As Maria sobbed, the tears freely flowed down her cheeks into her dress and on to the floor.

When the council returned from kpɔvi where they were supposed to have consulted the mythical old man called Amega Kpui, everything in the chapel went quiet, except for the buzzing sound that came from the lonely wasp flying high up near the rafters. Maria tried to read her fate from the looks on the faces of the councilors but they all kept shifting their glances. None could look directly into her eyes. Their faces could not yield much information. It was as if they had all donned ritual sacrifice masks made of steel. Then she saw on his father's face a smile, like a sudden rainbow bursting across a plain blue sky. Instantly, her whole being was flooded with renewed hope and strength. Her father's smile was the silver lining in the cloud she has been waiting for. She tried to smile back at her father but a sudden lump seemed to have appeared in her throat that seemed to choke her and prevent her from reciprocating her father's smile.

On the other hand, could it also be due to the noise Zerubabel Koklotsu made as he cleared his throat to address her?

"Maria Amedzro, daughter of Catechist of Yesukpodzi Christian Community," Zerubabel thundered. Maria looked squarely into his face, trying to outsmart him by catching the verdict from his eyes before he could let it fall off his lips. Unfortunately, the harder she looked, all she saw was her father's smile. There was a brief silence, then Zerubabel picked up the trail one more time. "The Church Council of Yesukpodzi herein assembled and sitting as a disciplinary body after much deliberation have found you..." Zerubabel paused, for what reason, nobody could tell. Maria felt her heart stop beating for a split second and the only thing that sustained her was the smile on her father's face. When her heart resumed its regular beat, it was as if some wild horses had been suddenly released to go on rampage inside her chest. At this point, she thought she saw Zerubabel smile at her. She quickly shifted her gaze to see whether the other councilors, now turned disciplinarians, were also carrying similar smiles. It was the moment Zerubabel chose to let out the dreaded words from his mouth. "...guilty of immorality of the extreme kind. You are therefore going to be..." Maria did not hear the rest.

Something snapped inside her when Zerubabel mentioned the word "guilty" and the whole chapel suddenly became pitch dark in her mind. Then she thought she heard a voice deep inside her cry out "O Zerubabel, what is this mountain I see before me?" Sister Abigail was the first to notice her going down but before she could shout "Mi le devia!" Zacheus Amedzro, the Catechist and father of Maria, had already sprung from his seat, jumped over three unoccupied wooden benches and a pew to his daughter's rescue. It was this quick reaction from the Catechist which prevented Maria from hitting the hard chapel floor. She was dazed. Sister Abigail quickly ran out and brought in a calabash of cold water. As the coldness of the water hit her face, whatever had snapped within her was restored. She could hear the echoes of the unrepentant voice of Zerubabel in a distance, continuing with his earlier pronouncement dispassionately, this time with renewed gusto. "You shall be taken outside by your father and handed over to the waiting crowd" he said, imperturbably, and took his seat. All this while, the Catechist was holding his daughter closer to himself, trying to support her.

At the mention of the crowd, Maria felt like fainting again but her father's grip on her was too firm to allow her to fall. He shook her up and doused her with more cold water. Maria wished the earth would rather open up and swallow her instead of going to face the dreaded crowd outside the chapel. "Oh Mawu...Mawu!" she gasped, as the tears poured down her cheeks. She wished all her free flowing tears gathered in one spot could make a pond large and deep enough to drown her. That, however, was not possible now.

"My daughter, the hour has come." The voice was very soft and tender. Maria looked up to see her father's face. He still wore the smile, the smile that continued to offer her some succour and assurance. The smile that indicated there was still hope and all wasn't lost. She took her father's hand in hers and gave it a gentle squeeze. Her father squeezed back in response. The two had found a medium to communicate silently. He held on to his daughter's hand a bit more firmly now than before. This, silent communication perhaps was to assure her that her father would not leave her when the time came. "I have a duty to perform. Please, assist me to perform it" her father said, still bearing the brave smile.

Maria understood him and promised herself she was not going to make her father's task any more difficult than it already was. She looked into her father's face, smiled back at him and said,

"Papa, I understand you. Carry on with your duty."

"Thank you, my daughter"

"But before you do so, I want you to believe me, that I have not known a man in my life. Papa, do you believe me?"

"Yes, my daughter, if nobody here will believe you, I, your father, believe you."

Maria and her father got into an embrace for a long time that obviously seemed to irritate the other councilors. When they came apart, there were no more tears in Maria's eyes. She gave her father her hand. He took it into his firm grip the way he promised his late wife, Maria's mother on her deathbed he would do on their daughter's wedding day. He promised his wife he was going to lead their daughter to the altar. Zacheus Amedzro, contrary to his dream and as cruel fate would have it, had to lead her only daughter and child rather to the slaughter. Nevertheless, before he gave her over, he presented her with a parting gift, a copy of the Holy Bible. Maria accepted the Bible, kissed it gently and held it close to her bosom. They had moved towards the doors of the chapel. The gates of the chapel swung open and Maria, standing by her father on top of the flight of cobbled stairs, looked down towards the entrance overlooking the chapel courtyard. The sight of the crowd wielding brooms and tree branches and the sudden eruption of the yelling that greeted her told her that she had come to the end of the road. She knew the magic of her father's smile would not save her. Perhaps, her Bible might. She tightened her grip on the holy book.

No sooner had the Catechist performed the traditional perfunctory Pontius Pilate hand-washing ritual and announced the verdict of the disciplinary council to the yelling crowd below than Maria was roughly dragged away from his side amidst hooting, insults and taunts into the middle of the crowd. Tears welled up in Zacheus' eyes. Red-hot tears no other person must see. For a man, they say, must never shed tears openly. These were tears he would never finish shedding. "Maria, Yehowa ne kplɔ wo dedie!" he murmured to himself and turned his weak footsteps homewards, away from the motley, madding throng that had his daughter captive. He would never know what happened to his daughter after handing her over. He was however certain Jehovah would listen to his last prayer and lead his daughter safely on her journey into the unknown. Maria was pushed ahead of the excited crowd that kept jeering at her. Soon, she began to taste the painful whipping of the brooms that swept her feet and footprints as she moved on towards the outskirts of Yesukpodzi where the Christian settlement shared an unofficial boundary with Akpadikɔfe.

On reaching the boundary, as they were wont to do by their Christian custom, the broom bearers moved forward, gave her one last resounding whipping with their brooms, gathered the dust swept around her feet and heaped it on her from head to toe. The leader of the women tied her broom around Maria's neck and gave her a final shove that was to send her crossing into the opposite side of the Christian settlement never to return. On the orders of the women's leader, the crowd that had accompanied Maria to the Yesukpodzi-Akpadikɔfe unofficial common territorial boundary gave out one final hoot and turned its back on Maria. She had become an outcast and no one was to turn and look at her twice. She had become an untouchable abomination. No one in the crowd returning from the boundary was to look back. It was feared anyone who disobeyed would suffer the punishment of Lot's wife. Perhaps, it was the fear of turning into a pillar of salt, more than anything else, that made the crowd run back immediately after pushing the outcast out of the territory of Yesukpodzi into Akpadikɔfe.

At the chapel, a special final cleansing ceremony was performed on each of them before they went to their various homes.

II

Te maliati, kae blane.

(The yam tendril that will not climb up the stake gets itself
entangled by wild vines.)

Long before the church elders had been officially notified,
almost every child in Akpadikɔfe knew of a scapegoat that
would be discharged and ostracized from Yesukpodzi on
the third Sunday after the coming full moon. This was not
surprising to most people since apart from the chief's gong-
gong beater the other reliable official source of information
was the rumour mill. As Sakpli put it whenever he was sober
and at his philosophical best, "Akpadikɔfe is a place where
like tiny mustard seeds, rumours watered by time germinate
and grow into giant trees burying their tap roots deep in the
hard but fertile soil of facts and truth." Even the elders of
Akpadikɔfe could not agree with him more on this. It might
have been for this reason that the children, under Sakpli's
leadership, defied the scorching midday sun and assembled in
readiness to mount a mock guard of honour for the Christian
outcast arriving through Akpadikɔfe from Yesukpodzi. "We
are going to continue from where our so-called Christian
brothers stopped",

Sakpli declared to his followers made up of mainly the youth and children of the town who responded with a loud yell of excitement. Most of the children looked quite scruffy and dirty from playing in the red earth in Akpadikɔfe. Except for one or two who had their mothers' cloths wrapped around themselves with the ends passing under their armpits and ending in a knot on their napes, most of them hardly had anything on. There were a few too who but for the tiny underwear sewn from empty flour bags they wore could be grouped with the others who were innocently naked as their little uncircumcised penises stuck out in front of their groins like maturing okro fruits hanging from the stalk. There were little girls too but they stood and watched proceedings from a respectable distance in the company of their mothers.

As Maria approached, Sakpli caused the children to line up on each side of the not-too-wide red earth street that ran east to west through the centre of the town. The children obeyed, and in no time at all the mock guard of honour to herald a Christian outcast from Yesukpodzi was ready.

Maria, her Bible firmly clutched under her arm with dirt all over her body, bravely walked through the column of children lined up on both sides of the narrow street. At a signal from Sakpli, the little children began to spit at her. Others pelted her with corn cobs and unripe akukɔ fruits. She made no effort at protecting her face which was already covered in dirt from the missiles being hurled at her. Some of the children went as far as touching her bulging tummy and taunting her with questions.

"Was it sweet?"
"Did you do it on a mat of reeds or on the bare floor?"
"Was it in the night or in the day time?"

And many more such silly questions. As she approached the end of the mounted guard, she saw a little boy dipping his hand into a pool of stagnant pool nearby and coming up with thick red mud which he held in readiness to fling at her. He was about to release the muddy missile when his eyes met those of the outcast. As if by some unseen power, the little boy's hand slowly fell limply to his side and the mud he had scooped dripped off to the ground at his feet.

Impulsively, Maria stopped by the little boy and looked him straight in the eyes. The next moment she saw tears running down his cheeks. Slowly, the little boy turned and started walking away from Maria's enquiring gaze. The little boy left his colleagues and the crowd to go and weep silently.

Maria felt some great relief after "inspecting" the mounted guard provided by the children of Akpadikɔfe. All she wished now was for her feet to carry her as fast as possible away. She did not care where. She only wished to be far away from the crowd.

She was getting her mind ready for the great ordeal ahead -wading through the crocodile-infested Gbaga River. It was a known fact that no outcast had ever waded through the river from one bank to the other safely. Maria knew there and then that her fate would be decided in that river. She had therefore planned to say a very short prayer at the bank of the river before stepping into its waters to become a sacrificial offering for the crocodiles. She was still rehearsing the prayer in her mind when she heard the sound of the bell. That might be the bell which, according to his father, was wrongfully appropriated from Yesukpodzi, by the people of Akpadikɔfe that the latter had insisted on keeping as war booty. Maria stood petrified. The momentary inner peace she thought she had gained was shattered and soon dissipated into nothingness by Sakpli's loud voice as he bellowed out the chant to the children. It was the tune of a well-rehearsed "chant of shame" specially composed by Sakpli to taunt Maria, and to announce her passage and progression through Akpadikɔfe. With an accompanying beat provided by sticks hitting rhythmically against empty kerosene tins, Sakpli shouted the beginning line of "the chant of shame":

"Chey-chey-il-chey-chey!"

"Eee-Yah!" came the response from the crowd of children. As if not satisfied with the verve with which the children responded to the call, "Commander" Sakpli decided to repeat it, this time, at the very top of his voice, so all could hear.

"Chey-chey-li-chey-chey!"

"Eee-Yah!" The response was thunderous and deafening and could be heard at the very end of the town.Efɔ gbɔme fu", he went on, according to the beat.

"Eee-Yah!" The crowd responded along the rhythmic pattern.

"Wo menya 'mekae doe o "Ee-Yah"

Efo Kodjo Mawugbe

"Wo ntɔ dzi natsɔe" "Ee Yah!"

"Maria do gbɔto lo o"

"Yee ... Akpadiviwoe midzrado, Maria gbɔna!"

Sakpli repeated the last but one line of the chant and everyone around took up the refrain once more.

"Yeeeee...Akpadiviwo midrzrado Maria gbɔna!"

The poor outcast from Yesukpodzi knew the worst was not over yet. Fate had only toyed with her the way a cat does with a mouse before finally killing it. The bell kept clanging rhythmically against the shrill and excited voices of the children as they stamped their feet and marched ruggedly after Maria with the chant of shame. The crowd begun to swell. What had originally commenced as a children's game of fun had virtually been taken over by the adults. To them, it was their chance to hit back at what they termed the hypocrisy of their Christian rivals. The crowd, now swollen and bursting with excitement, thronged behind the outcast as she sauntered doggedly along the Western end of Akpadikɔfe, towards the banks of the Gbaga River. She tried to quicken her steps in order to keep some respectable distance between her and the noisy crowd. It was as if she had lead tied to the soles of her feet. She tried one more time to quicken her steps but ended up fumbling and falling flat on her face in the dusty street.

The crowd cheered in wild excitement. She was so exhausted and could not hurriedly gather herself up from the dust. When she finally did, there was no more energy left in her. Like an old woman returning from a distant farm, she plodded on weariedly towards the destiny that awaited her on the bank of Gbaga.

Everybody wanted to be at the bank of Gbaga to witness the climax of the ordeal. Nobody wanted to be told about it. They all wanted to see things for themselves. For most of them it was going to be their first time. The last time an outcast was torn into pieces by the crocodiles of Gbaga was many years back, as far as any living memory could recollect. It was in the year Amega Lovi, the chief fisherman, was born. It was said that his mother had gone to witness an outcast torn to pieces but when the crocodiles finally appeared, it frightened her so much that she went into labour and instantly gave birth prematurely at the riverside. People nicknamed him Lovi - child of the crocodile. For this reason, pregnant women were barred from witnessing such occasions. Maria and the crowd led by Sakpli and his children's brigade finally arrived at the riverside having done the four or so kilometers journey in a little over two hours. At a signal from Sakpli, the parade commander, the crowd gave a loud, long shout from the very floor of their bowels. Others splashed water on her. Then the bell rang for a long time. When it stopped, everything else ceased. The birds in the forest would not chirp. The wind would not blow and all the trees nearby stood still. The only discernible noise came from the waters of Gbaga falling off some rocks in the distance, mingled with the sound of Maria's sobbing. The crowd waited and watched with bated breath.

Maria walked to the edge of the river. She went down on her knees, offered a short prayer, made the sign of the cross and boldly stepped forward. She sent her right foot first. As it touched the water, she felt the coldness wrap around her ankle and bite deep into it with its liquid teeth. Then she noticed the rings that kept expanding in concentric circles to cover the disturbed surface of the water. A cold shudder shot up through her whole frame. She pressed her right foot harder until she was sure it had touched solid ground beneath the water. Then, she brought her left foot down into the water but this time she had gotten used to the river's chilling effect. She stood for a while, made sure her feet were planted on a solid base beneath the water. She pressed the Bible to her bosom with one hand and began her favourite song, the orphan's cry, a song she had been taught at Sunday School when she was a little girl.

"*Afetɔ... Afetɔ Xɔnam xɔnam dzro Xɔnam dzro!...*"
Indeed, the poor orphan needed the Lord's deliverance.
"*Mede ku ku...!*" *She pleaded with the good Lord.*
"*Tsyɔevi le xli dzii!*
Tsyɔevi le xli dzii!"
Hear the orphan cry, Lord, please hearken to the voice of a poor helpless, hapless orphan. She waded on. The water level climbed up to her knees and still kept rising as she waded further in.

The large crowd on the bank behind her kept quiet and looked on as the water level climbed up to her thighs.

"Nye Mawu-e-e-e-!
Dem kaba,
Afetɔ ne dem kaba"

My Lord, deliver the poor orphan without delay. The water level now was about her waistline and the force of the current was increasing. She could be swept off her feet if she was not careful. Maria was so engrossed in her song that she did not realise she was approaching the part of Gbaga where the currents were noted for their roughness and swiftness. She did not even hear the sudden thunderous cheers from the crowd on the bank behind her. When she first spotted the objects on the surface of the river, she thought they were floating pieces of logs. Then she seemed to have noticed the snout and the hidden glassy eyes inside the hideous slits. That was when it dawned on her those couldn't be floating logs. They were crocodiles. She counted three of them.

Maria knew her end had come. The amphibians closed in on her and started swimming in a circle with Maria at the center. She kept wading on, even as the water level rose above her chest forcing her to lift the hand holding the Bible high up above her head to prevent it from getting wet. As Maria kept wondering what the crocodiles were going to do next, there came a long, loud shout from the crowd on the bank that tore through the silence of the forest. Maria looked upstream where she saw another set of crocodiles cruising aggressively towards her. They were six in number. Six large crocodiles coming to join in the impending onslaught. At least that was what everyone around thought. This was indeed a rare sight and the crowd standing at the bank had every reason to be ecstatic.

Normally, it was only three crocodiles that came to devour an outcast. In the case of Maria, there were a total of nine. This, more than any thing else, left no doubt in the minds of many onlookers about the enormity of Maria's sin and the fact that they were beyond remission.

Maria refused to be intimidated by the number of crocodiles parading around her. Crocodiles or not, she must sing on. And she indeed sang her own modified version asking for deliverance from the hungry crocodiles.

"Afetɔ ne dem kaba tso lovi wo sime Afetɔ ne dem kaba tso lovi wo si me Afetɔ ne dem kaba tso lovi wo sime"

She continued to sing the refrain of her Sunday school song as she waded through the river with the water level climbing steadily. Suddenly, the first three crocodiles that formed the inner circle around Maria opened their jaws to display their frightening chainsaw-like set of teeth. Like Maria, the crowd knew the end was near. The other six crocodiles tried to reach Maria but seemed to be having a hard time breaking through the inner circle that had been formed by the first three. Maria kept on singing as the water rose above her chest to her neck. Suddenly she lost her foothold. Apparently, she had inadvertently stepped on a slippery rock. She fell into the river. All the nine crocodiles vanished from the surface of the river. The crowd on the bank cheered in excitement as it kept scanning the surface of the water for floating torn limbs and blood.

The crocodiles that formed the inner ring were the first to surface, followed later in quick succession by the six others. It was quite later that Maria emerged, hand first, still clutching her Bible, now soaked. She looked quite frightened. Maria picked up the thread of the song where she had left off and kept moving on with great caution. She realised the bank ahead was getting closer and closer whilst the water level was receding gradually. Would she be able to make it there? Would her feet ever touch the dry bank on the other side of Gbaga? As Maria drew closer to the bank, the crowd behind her became more anxious. However, the elderly among the crowd remained calm. They were aware of the behavioural instincts of some of these amphibious predators that allowed them to toy with their prey to a point where the prey would think they had gained their freedom only to be whipped back into the water with the strong tails of the predators and devoured. Some of the elders had seen it before and were therefore not going to be troubled by Maria's nearness to the bank. As far as they were concerned, no outcast had ever survived and outlived the test of the crocodiles in the Gbaga River and no one would. So solid were their convictions in this respect that even when the nine crocodiles broke ranks and swam back the way they had come and Maria had gone down on her knees on dry land at the other bank of Gbaga to offer thanks to her Lord and Maker, they still thought the amphibians were going to make a sudden u-turn for the final attack. When at last it dawned on them they would see the crocodiles and the outcast no more, their jaws dropped in awe and utter disbelief. As far as the elders were concerned, something had to be wrong. The gods needed to be consulted for an explanation of this unprecedented occurrence.

Maria got up from her knees and turned round slowly to the bank where she had come from. The crowd was still gathered there. They were like dark dots in the distance. The water and the tears in her eyes could not make her see clearly from that distance. Yet, she thought a face flashed through her mind. Yes, it was that little boy. The little boy who could not hurl the mud at her... The little boy who... Then it clicked. A clear picture with date, time and place began to form a discernible pattern in her mind. It was as if she had succeeded in locating that one missing piece required to complete the jigsaw puzzle. 'Yes, the note from Kɔkuvi a couple of months back before he flew out of the country to pursue further studies. That was the little boy who secretly handed the note to her after church service one Sunday on the blind side of her father. It was the note in which Kɔkuvi had proposed friendship to her and announced he was going to pay her a visit one evening. When that evening came, she feigned sick and did not accompany her father to the all-night prayer session at church. So that was Kɔkuvi's little brother. Maria, for the first time, smiled to herself and remembered the manner of her father's smile. She wished someone could run and tell her father the crocodiles had vindicated her.

However, it would not be until the third day after her ordeal with the crocodiles when the congregation had not seen her father the Catechist in public that a delegation would be sent to his house. The door to his room was barred from within. The stench emerging from there was quite pungent. The door was forced open. His bloated body, tongue drooping, was still dangling by the neck on a twine fastened to the rafters. Close to his dangling feet and lying on its side, was the metal bucket he had upturned, stood upon and kicked to do the dastardly deed. Some men were hired from Akpadikɔfe to cut the rope to let down the corpse and wrap it up in some old calico and straw mat. The oozing decomposing body was hurriedly conveyed to the beniglah reserved for people who died ignobly. There, it was interred in a shallow, unmarked grave.

Beniglah belongs to that cluster of words in the Ewe vocabulary that intrigue many people as to its origin. According to Sakpli, it is the corrupted version of the English words 'burial ground'. Nobody would mourn and nobody would ever commemorate the passing away of the hard working catechist who became a victim of the uncompromising high moral standards he insisted upon among the youth of his congregation. Maria would always remember her father for his smile but would never know how he died or where and how he was buried.

Slowly, Maria turned her back to Yesukpodzi, Akpadikɔfe, the crowd on the other bank of Gbaga and directed her footsteps on to the narrow footpath and walked into the outstretched arms of the jungle, where some wild animal might pounce on her and bring to full closure this unbearable ordeal that had become her lot.

III

Fodo me gbe a kana o.

(The hungry belly does not refuse to take the least that is offered it.)

For the first time in the collective memory of Akpadikɔfe, a crowd had gone to witness an outcast torn to pieces by the goddess of the river but had returned home with torn minds. Wide fissures of doubts begun to show on the hitherto solid walls of confidence people had in the river goddess. Serious questions were raised as to why the crocodiles did not devour the poor Christian outcast. The conduct and reputation of Bokɔ Akatsa, the gatekeeper of the shrine of the river goddess, was called into question. Some said he had wronged the goddess and needed to confess to the community. Many stories were hurriedly fabricated in an orchestrated effort to explain away the unprecedented phenomenon whose interpretation still defied the wisdom and intelligence of the gray heads of Akpadikɔfe.

One story had it that the outcast was a witch who succeeded in casting a spell on the crocodiles. Another one said she was able to scare away the crocodiles with the Bible she held in her hand. As if to give more credence to her Christian background as the source of her feat, certain people claimed they saw a halo of light in the form of a giant crucifix suspended as if from the sky over Maria's head as she went through the river. Somebody said she thought she saw a figure of a strange man in all white apparel lift Maria out of the water and both of them walked on the surface of the water to the opposite bank.

This last story was quickly discounted by the elders of Akpadikɔfe as pure fabrication. Unfortunately, it was that story more than any crusade or evangelistic activity that won new converts from far and near into the church at Yesukpodzi. Many were those who believed the incident was proof of Maria's innocence in the eyes of the river goddess. The bigger argument confronting the whole of Akpadikɔfe was that if indeed the young girl was innocent, then who was guilty? Some said it was the community and by extension its leadership that was guilty and needed to pacify itself and the goddess of Gbaga. In other words, Chief Korku Adovor and his elders needed to take steps to pacify the aggrieved goddess. Instead of admitting their guilt and purging themselves as required by custom, these elders resorted to finger-pointing in other directions away from themselves. Among them came a group circulating the story that Maria had indeed been killed by the crocodiles. Their explanation was that the crocodiles had gone back on land to conduct a search and destroy mission in which Maria had been located, dragged back into the river and killed. What was required now was proof of the death of the outcast. They were therefore looking for volunteers who would swim across the river to the other bank in search of the mortal remains of Maria. Among the people who believed in this story was Korku Adovor, Chief of Akpadikɔfe.

Seven full moons had gone past since Maria successfully waded through the crocodile-infested Gbaga from one bank to the other. Sakpli was relaxing in front of his hut one fine evening chewing tiger nuts dipped in salt water when the chief's messengers, numbering five in all, arrived to have a word with him. The chief and his elders had decided to send an expedition to wade through the river from one bank to the other to ascertain whether indeed the crocodiles did or did not devour Maria Amedzro. It had been decided at the palace that emissaries be sent to Sakpli if he would be willing to volunteer to lead the fact-finding expedition. Sakpli, after listening to them suddenly burst into laughter, forcing the fine granulated particles of tiger-nut chaff in his mouth to go out in a spray into the faces of the three palace messengers who unfortunately found themselves seated right in front of him. Although it was most unintentional, the way Sakpli laughed loud and long and did not even bother to offer apologies for spraying his visitors made the messengers think otherwise. The visitors wiped their faces with the loose ends of their cloth and the back of their hands.

"Did you people say it is the chief of Akpadikɔfe who sent you to enquire from me if I would volunteer to serve as a Team Leader of the fact-finding expedition?"

"Yes, he sent us," chorused the five men. There was a long silence.

"I will tell you a very interesting story," Sakpli began. "This search for volunteers for the fact-finding expedition reminds me of an interesting story my grandfather told me when I was a little boy." He paused and tossed a few more tiger nuts into his mouth and set his jaws crushing them.

When the messengers who were sitting directly in front of him noticed this, they quickly shifted positions lest they became innocent victims of another spraying session. As far as they were concerned, Sakpli was only replenishing his armoury, so they needed to stay on the side of caution and out of firing range. Sakpli smiled to himself as he watched them shift sitting positions.

"Once upon a time..." he begun his story in earnest but again paused, this time to savour and swallow the milky tiger nut juice that had collected in his mouth. "In the ancient kingdom of Nɔtsie, where the great Agɔkɔli ruled his people with iron fists, there lived a loan shark by name Amega Vidzraku. He was a very popular money-lender known throughout the neighbouring clans, villages and towns, from the creeks of Badagry through Kutornu to Aflao and even beyond. His popularity did not have to do so much with his wealth but rather with the excessive interests his loans attracted and the cruel punishment he inflicted on defaulters. He had a very efficient horse-riding debt-collector by name Ahmadou from the ancient Kingdom of Sokoto. Ahmadou was all muscles and bones and very little brain. It was said that once he caused a defaulting debtor to be tied by rope to

75

his horse and dragged for miles on the ground to serve as a deterrent to all who owed his master. At a glance, Ahmadou looked like a badly carved giant wooden mask. A long ugly looking scar ran from just above his left eye down across his left cheek, slicing his upper lip into two unequal halves creating a window through which a few of the upper row of teeth seemed to draw in fresh air and peep at the world. His ears jutted out as if they wanted to fly away from his head. Moreover,his head was scalp shaven and smeared with shea butter, giving it a perpetual glittering look under the tropical sun. He always walked about bare-chested, displaying his dark ebony skin and over blown biceps. He stood almost seven feet tall with thick long arms that ended in broad oar-like palms" Sakpli carefully spewed the chaff in his mouth and took in fresh tiger nuts. "That is indeed an awe-inspiring son of a man you have just described" remarked the leader of the messengers.

"Yes, indeed," concurred Sakpli. "Such a man could draw the ropes of the asabu fishing net single-handed," said another. They all laughed and Sakpli continued with his narrative.

"This was Amega Vidzraku's muscle man. Each time a man came to borrow money from him, he would send for Ahmadou to come and stand by his side. 'You see this man', Vidzraku would say to the prospective borrower, pointing at Ahmadou. The would-be-borrower seldom opened his mouth and would only nod in answer as he watched Ahmadou crack his knuckles very loudly in his presence. 'Good, if you fail to meet the agreed terms of repayment, I shall ask this man here to pay you a courtesy call. I hope you understand' "More often than not, the full import of the veiled threat got branded in the subconscious of the would-be-borrower long before Vidzraku finished his statement. Most people who failed to pay their loans on time had their children or relations seized and dragged to work like slaves on Vidzraku's farms for as long as the payment was outstanding." Sakpli paused and took in a fresh breath of air to relax his vocal chords to spice up the narrative and make it sound more conversational.

"Well, it so happened that a man from far away Igbobi noted in his town for non-payment of debts came to the ancient kingdom of Notsie to collect a huge loan from Amega Vidzraku. When he defaulted payment and Ahmadou was dispatched to recover the money with accrued interest, do you know what happened?"

"No, we don't," all the messengers said in excited unison. This was a certain sign to Sakpli that the messengers were hearing the story for the first time. He was therefore going to take his time to give it some dramatic embellishment to make his guests to enjoy it the more. He tossed a few more tiger nuts into his mouth but had to quickly let them out because he smelt one rotten nut in there that did not taste right. As he selected fresh nuts to toss into his mouth, he asked the messengers,

"Do you want to know?"

"Of course we do" they replied with the eagerness akin to

pupils in *abɔdzokpo* caught up in the intriguing web of a teacher's folktale.

"I will tell you. Relax... The debtor from Igbobi said to Ahmadou 'Look here, my friend, I am not used to paying my debts on time. I am a habitual defaulter from birth. You can ask anybody in Igbobi town. When I borrow money, I pay when I feel like. So, go back to Nɔtsie and tell your master what I have told you.' The messengers burst into laughter. Sakpli allowed them the liberty to do so, at least for now, before picking up the trail one more time.

"Then Ahmadou in his thunderous voice roared 'I am not going back to my master without the money. I have never gone back to him from a debt-collecting errand without taking to him his money or the debtor. You can check my records from Badagry to Aflao and even beyond. So, you either pay up or I offer you a not too comfortable ride from here to Nɔtsie.' 'Are you deaf? I say I won't pay now!' retorted the debtor from Igbobi. 'And I, Ahmadou Sokoto say, by Allah, you are going to pay here and now' the debt collector roared louder than before."

"Today is today" One of the messengers who obviously had been completely carried away by the story remarked. "Yes, indeed today is the day we are going to see which of the two water pots can contain more water than the others," another messenger remarked.

"That is so, ze wu ze..." concurred the leader of the messengers. Sakpli only nodded and smiled.

"Well, as they were screaming at each other 'I won't pay now... You will pay now... I won't pay now...You will pay now', Ofufulifu, the village lunatic appeared on the scene and asked to know what the matter was. After listening to both sides, all Ofufulifu could say was 'Hmmm, this load is too heavy for me to carry alone. I shall need someone else to hear your story.'

'Whether another person comes to hear my story or not, I stand by what I have said. I am not paying my debt today. Go and come back another day.' The debtor from Igbobi declared aggressively. 'You are a big joker. I am going make sure you pay today and no other day,' said Ahmadou, as he cracked his knuckles loudly. There was momentary silence. The debtor and the debt collector stood face to face, staring down at each other, eyeball-to-eyeball, waiting for the first man to make the next move. None of them would blink. Ofufulifu looked on with great ardor. Very slowly, the debtor from Igbobi first drew a sharp, ugly-looking dagger from under his garment. Not wishing to be outdone, Ahmadou also drew an even longer and sharper knife from a scabbard hidden under his gown. They both stood watching each other with daggers drawn. Whilst Ofufulifu looked on completely bemused as to which of the two men would make that first fatal move, the debtor from Igbobi spoke.

'You say you want to collect your master's money. All right, here it is, take it.' As the man from Igbobi said 'Take it', he with one deft movement plunged the dagger into his own belly and fell face down on it'

"Ao!" gasped the attentive messengers.

"Yes, within minutes, the Igbobi debtor was dead." Sakpli spoke with a feigned touch of sorrow in his voice. "Then

Ahmadou said to the corpse lying on the ground 'My friend, don't think you are going to escape with my master's money. I shall chase you even to the ends of the earth to collect it.' So saying, Ahmadou held his long knife to his navel and with one swift movement of the arm, the instrument found itself buried to the hilt in his belly.

The noise from his fall was as if a giant tree had been blown to the ground in a heavy thunderstorm." Sakpli kept quiet for a while, either as his way of observing a moment of silence for the departed characters in his story or just to allow the foolishness of the tragedy he had recounted to sink deep into the minds of his audience. He spewed the tiger nut chaff that had collected in his mouth on to the ground around his feet.

"So, they both died," remarked the leader of the messengers. "Yes, they died but that is not the end of the story." Sakpli flung a few more tiger nuts into his mouth and set his jaws to grind them in copious meticulousness. "Ofufulifu, in whose presence all these things were unfolding, felt so intrigued and wished to know how the matter would be brought to full closure. He wished to know what would transpire on the other side of life and whether Ahmadou would be able to collect the debt or the Igbobi man would still refuse to pay.

As if seized by some sprit, Ofufulifu started screaming 'Wait for me Ahmadou, I am coming with you! Please wait for me!' He pushed Ahmadou's corpse onto its side and pulled out the blood stained dagger embedded in its body. Without bothering to wipe it clean, Ofufulifu buried it in his own tummy and fell down on Ahmadou's corpse. Dead!" All the messengers burst out into laughter at the comical twist to what might have been an interesting thought-provoking tragedy. When Sakpli thought his audience from his chief's palace had laughed enough, he tried to wheedle them to find out which of the three characters in his story was the most stupid and why. It was agreed, after a some warm exchanges and counter arguments that Ofufulifu the village lunatic was the most stupid of the three. Their reason was that the matter for which he killed himself had nothing to do with him. It was completely none of his business. "Very good, I also agree with you that Ofufulifu was the most stupid of the three idiots" Sakpli said softly and thought by now the messengers from the palace would have gotten the drift of his conversation. The look on their faces however, did not really show they had any clue whatsoever. Yet, these were supposed to be elders advising the chief in his palace. Pitiful though it might seem, Sakpli was prepared to spend some time to educate these messengers a little more at no extra cost.

"Now, with regards to the fact-finding expedition you were asked to see me about, hear my response. I am prepared to lead the expedition if and only if Chief Korku Adovor and his good-for-nothing wives and children will agree to be part of the expedition team." The messengers were completely dumbfounded. They could not believe what they were hearing. "Go tell that chief of yours that I may be a drunkard but I am not Ofufulifu. I am not stupid! I don't have lunacy or epilepsy running through my family." "That is an insult

you are asking us to carry to the chief, you know that?"
"And what do you call that which he parcelled up nicely for
you to carry to me on your stupid heads? A compliment?"

There was silence. "Tell him, I say if he eats shit, Sakpli is
not willingly to be part of those he invites to share in it. I do
not eat shit. And even if, taflatse, I must eat shit, I will eat my
own and not that of some lazy, good-for-nothing, useless,
impotent chief."
"How dare you, Sakpli!" roared the leader of the messengers.
"You have crossed the line of no return. The chief will hear
of this," said one of the messengers very loudly. "Of course,
they are meant for the ears of the deaf and dumb thief of
a chief of yours. So, carry every word to him. *Avu koklo...
kaabli!*"

The messengers would not let him finish his insults. They
hurriedly got up and scampered out of Sakpli's compound.

That very night, Sakpli packed the few valuables he treasured
most, set his own compound ablaze and fled Akpadikɔfe. He
ensured he had handed over the controversial church bell
back to its rightful owners at Yesukpodzi, maybe as a sign
of pacification for his past, before making his way into exile.
He sought refuge in Sakabo, where he offered and pledged
whatever was left of his skills and talents in exchange for
citizenship and security to the palace of Torgbui Ashi Aklama
I, a bitter rival of Korku Adovor, chief of Akpadikɔfe.

FIFTH LEG

*Bometsilae dea dɔ deka gbe
zigbɔzi eve.*

(It is the fool who runs the same
errand twice.)

True to Togbuiga's prediction, Sakpli woke up feeling hungry. Before he could ask for food, a bowl of steaming *akple* and *bɔbi tadi* was set on a low table before him. He ate it thankfully. At the end of it, he let out a loud belch that set Adevu barking at him. This dog had been lying at the base of the table very close to Sakpli's feet hoping for crumbs to fall from Sakpli's hand on to the ground. From time to time, it wagged its tail to brush Sakpli's feet as if to remind him of its presence. Each time Sakpli took a morsel towards his mouth, Adevu lifted its head wishing the morsel would fall from Sakpli's fingers to the ground. "Your prayers will not be answered. Your colleagues are in the bush hunting for game and you are comfortably ensconced here, under a kitchen table, praying for morsels of akple to accidentally drop from these hungry fingers of mine. Such accidents rarely happen these days", Sakpli said to the dog, as he swept the bottom of the plate containing the abɔbi with the last morsel of akple which he swallowed with a loud gulp. He called out to whoever was around to come and clear the table. No sooner had the table been cleared than Adevu crawled out and crossed over to lie next to the entrance of the kitchen.

"That would be better for you," intoned Sakpli, as he observed Adevu change its location. Surprisingly, Adevu turned and barked back at Sakpli as if it had heard and

understood the drunkard's last statement. This shook Sakpli
a little bit. According to the people's belief, if a dog barked
at a person who had belched after a meal, it was considered
a bad omen. It portended evil. That is what the sages said.
Some believed it. Others did not. But Sakpli was not a man to
give in to baseless superstitious beliefs. He let out a second
belch, called for a calabash of water, which he drank in noisy
gulps and started rubbing his hand on his stomach. Adevu
barked again in the direction of Sakpli. The drunkard smiled
teasingly at the dog and said, "Now, I am ready to leave for
Sakplikɔfe, my cottage. But I must first see Torgbuiga to
thank him for his boundless hospitality. He has really fed
me well."

"Torgbuiga is busy in his chamber. You can go home. I'll
convey your message to him later", said Apedomeshie, the
elder wife and head of the servants in the women's quarters
who had arrived to offer Sakpli a piece from a broom for a
tooth pick.

"Nobody conveys my message to Torgbuiga when I know
I can have unimpeded access to his ears in his own palace.
I shall be the conveyor of my own message. There shall be
no third party involvement. I know my rights." Sakpli said
authoritatively.

"What is it again…?Who is making trouble for my good
friend?" asked Torgbuiga as he stepped in unnoticed through
a side door from behind. "Nobody is making trouble for him
my lord. He says he wants to see you and I asked him to pass
on whatever message he has for you through me and…,"
Apedomeshie explained.

"This friend here is special. He speaks to me directly. He has my ears any day," said Torgbuiga.

"Mother of the palace, I hope you heard my vindication from the lips of His Royal Highness" Sakpli replied, looking with squinted eyes in the direction of Apedomeshie with a mischievous 'didn't-I-tell-you' smile on his face.

"Now that I know he has your ears any day, I shall no longer come between you and his big ears", Apedomeshie responded, without bothering to look in the direction of Sakpli.

"Mother of the palace, I take that reference to my ears as a royal compliment from His Royal Highness' chief cook, who just fed me well. If some other person, I mean a nonentity, someone of no royal lineage and with no fixed address, had made such a reference, I would have engaged the one in a fight to redeem the honour of my ears."

Torgbuiga burst into a bout of laughter. Apedomeshie looked Sakpli up and down, heaved a sigh and said

"You are simply incurable." and walked away from the two men.

"Well, my friend, is there anything else you want to see me about?" Torgbuiga asked, after he had recovered from the laughter.

"Indeed, your Highness," replied Sakpli, as he looked around furtively as if to make sure no one else was listening.

"But it must be out of earshot of these inquisitive women here", he whispered conspiratorially to Torgbuiga.

"I think I agree with you. Shall we go in then?"

Torgbuiga led the way into one of the many chambers of the palace where they hoped to sit and talk without any intrusion or eavesdropping by anyone. No sooner had the door been shut behind Torgbuiga and his friend than the women around burst into laughter. It was common knowledge that people who came seeking special audience with Torgbuiga and ended up with him behind closed doors were loan-seekers. The palace women who had observed the behavior of Sakpli ever since he arrived at the palace that morning were convinced he was no exception. They prayed Torgbuiga would see through his subterfuge and not grant him any loan because Sakpli would end up "drinking the money," as the locals often put it.

Sixth Leg

*Gafodokui mefoa avlimeyigbega
na ame o.*

(Your watch can tell you the time
of the day but not the time of your
death.)

Efo Kodjo Mawugbe

It was evening and the tropical sun, now a mild glowing yellow ball was plastered against the western sky behind the distant coconut trees whose shadows provided welcome shades along the periphery of the lagoon. The portion of the shadows that extended into the water seemed to dance to the rhythm of the disturbed surface of the water. Akuyovi and her other colleagues were returning from the weekly Dabala market in a single file through the narrow bush path towards the lagoon where they would be ferried in canoes across to Tɔgodo. From here, they would be joined by other traders from the Dzalele and Kɔjoviakɔfe markets and, as a group now trek the ten kilometre path to Sakabo. Klogo the hunter was relaxing in an easy chair outside on the verandah, next to the door to his bedroom. The main gate to the compound was secured. It was that season of the year when hunters took a mandatory break to allow the forest animals to have some breathing and breeding space.

It was the season hunters polished and oiled their hunting rifles. Klogo was busily cleaning and fixing the parts of the rifle he had dismantled earlier in the day. Akuyovi, his wife, who has just returned from the market, had placed a bowl containing roasted corn and salted pieces of dried coconut beside him on a low kitchen table, He was chewing wuya-wuya as he went about refitting those delicate screws back on the rifle. From time to time, he looked up at the sun. It was now a big ball of orange gradually sliding its way across the sky to take refuge behind the hills, where it would sleep to wake up from the opposite direction the next day. Klogo wondered how the sun performed that magic of going to bed in the West and rising in the East. He wished someone would explain it to him.

From time to time, he deliberately shut his eyes and allowed his whole body and all of his senses to savour the taste the of coconut and the salted roasted corn on his tongue as the mixture slid down his gullet sending his Adam's apple into short up-and-down movements. He cleaned the barrel of the rifle and lifted it to peep through to see if there was any speck of dirt hiding somewhere. He had lifted it and aimed it at the setting sun when he heard a loud knock on the main gate to his compound. He dropped his aim and called out.
"Akuyovi"
"Yes, my lord"
"I know you just returned from the market and must be feeling tired, but there is someone outside our gate. See who it is."
"Yes, my lord."

Instantly, she stopped whatever she was doing in the kitchen and dashed towards the main gate.

Klogo was still wondering who might be calling on him at such time of day when Akuyovi returned from the gate. "It is Torgbuiga's Tsami and two others. He says he has a message for you. Should I allow them in?"

"A messenger of the chief commands the same respect as the one who sent him. Sure, let them in."

"Yes, my Lord," said Akuyovi as she hurried back to the gate to let the visitors in. Before she returned with the emissaries from the palace, her husband had crossed over to bring one of the benches nearby and moved his easy chair to set it under the akukɔ tree. The gate opened and in stepped three men. It was the Tsami from the Ashi Aklama royal house, flanked on each side by a palace attendant. The Tsami of course carried his distinct symbol of office, a five foot high gold-plated staff, at the top of which sat the figures of two people sitting at a table sharing a meal from the same bowl. This was supposed to represent trust and love, the communal spirit of sharing which the people of Sakabo treasured.

"The maggot that lives inside the red hot pepper..." Tsami began as soon as his feet touched the threshold of Klogo's compound and sighted the hunter in his seat.

"...And yet never complains the pepper is hot," Klogo completed the proverb for him and tossed in one of his own. "The housefly says life is made up of the future and history, that's why it washes both its front and hind legs."

"Indeed the housefly is right. The elders have maintained that it is looking back that gives the future colour." Tsami was displaying his complete understanding of the proverb. "You see, my brother, it is good, as the sages say, on gaining every station in life's progressive day, to pause a little while in contemplation and mark the travelled path," Klogo continued.

"Because in life, we find the past foreshadowing what will be, much as it reminds us of what had been," concluded Tsami and proved once again that his wit has not gone blunt. Tsami further understood the double-edged meaning of what the old hunter meant by that particular proverb. He knew where the sting was hidden in the proverb.

The old hunter was trying to rake an old wound. It has to do with something that happened in the past between the two of them. Just the two of them. An old rivalry that each of them tried to downplay whenever they met. He therefore decided to counter it before its full import could be discerned by his two attendants.

"The Tsitsiawo have said that when that same house fly performs a feat worthy of emulation, it ceases to be called a mere housefly, its name changes to Togbato, the tsetsefly," Tsami continued to display the fact that he was still a force to reckon with when it came to proverbs.

"That is correct, but let's not waste our energies on mere houseflies", Klogo felt his old adversary was gaining the upper hand. He needed to redirect the conversation into other areas that would leave him rather in firm control of affairs.

"Maybe you want us to talk about the tortoise then, I mean yourself." Tsami said sardonically. "Maybe, the tortoise would give us more food for thought than a mere housefly" Klogo conceded. "The tortoise says it is really dancing hard but its hard shell makes it impossible for onlookers to realise the vigour with which it is dancing."

"Tell the tortoise to keep on trying." Klogo responded, making everyone laugh.

"But remember, I am still the Klogo, the tortoise that the eagle can not prey upon in spite of its sharp talons and strong hooked beak."

It was while they were laughing that Tsami thought he noticed Klogo's jaw moving up and down.
"Hey, my friend, are you still eating?" Tsami queried jokingly.
"As the goat says, the jaw that remains idle becomes an easy target for the devil to use in idle gossip." Klogo responded.
"So the old hunter decides to use his jaw as a corn mill to grind roasted corn and salted coconut for his stomach, whilst protecting his mouth from engaging in idle gossips," Tsami riposted and everyone including Klogo broke into laughter again. After a brief silence, each of the visitors took a position on the bench provided by the old hunter under the akukɔ tree.
"Will the old hunter be kind enough to open his mouth for us to examine how well his corn mill has worked on the stuff in his mouth?" asked one of Tsami's attendants, who also felt the need to have his voice heard. Klogo waited for them to finish laughing before throwing in his picturesque response.
"If it is said that the cat has soiled its anus, it is not for the mouse to verify it" They were suddenly thrown into another fit of laughter that kept each one of them wondering where and how Klogo often came up with such apt and precise

proverbs. Akuyovi arrived with a large calabash filled with water for her husband's guests. It was offered first to Tsami who took a sip and passed it on to the man on his right. After sipping a little, he passed it to his colleague seated at the left of Tsami who also took a sip and poured some on the ground before handing the calabash back to Akuyovi with thanks. Akuyovi took the calabash and made her way back towards the kitchen where she would remain until her husband sent for her.

"Why, but you didn't drink my water" queried Klogo in feigned anger. The journey from Torgbuiga's palace to your house isn't like from Kutornu to Aflao for which a man shall need water." replied Tsami.

"Are you sure? Don't forget the crocodile lives in water yet it still drinks water."

"That is so, but when one's stomach is so full of solid matter, you'll agree with me water hardly finds immediate space in there to occupy". Tsami, now convinced that the atmosphere had been relaxed and made conducive enough for civil discourse, decided to take charge of affairs.

"Can we greet you now?"

"The path is clear. You may proceed"

Tsami and his two companions got into a squatting position as a sign of respect as they offerred their greetings.

"Receive good evening"

"Good evening... and the people of your house?" "They are fine"

"Your wives?"

"They are awake"

"Your children?"

"They are alive."

At this point, Klogo intentionally allowed the mandatory, customary time-honoured split-second pause to enable the respondent to come to the top, as it were, and steer the course of the greetings.

"And the people of your compound?"

"*Mawu* has given us today". responded Klogo.

"And your wife?"

"She is alive"

Tsami was considerate enough to steer the greetings away from enquiring about Klogo's children. For a man who has been married for more than fifteen years without a child, any such reference would seem like a deliberate poking of his wound. Moving from a squatting to a standing position, the men shook hands with one another, each handshake terminating in a loud, snapping of the fingers in the usual male fashion.

"*Miawoe zɔ ka-ka-ka-ka,*" Klogo welcomed them.

"*Ayooo!*" the guests responded in unison.

Having welcomed his guests formally, Klogo proceeded to enquire of their mission.

"As you can see, I have just finished my evening meal and was whiling away the time cleaning my hunting gun when you burst into my compound unannounced like some mercenaries. If you wouldn't mind, may I know what pursues you into my house?"

"Tsami, are you there?" asked the one selected to relay the message.

"Speak, for I am all ears," Tsami responded.

"A question has been thrown to us. The lord of this house requires of us our mission"

Tsami cleared his throat and began. "First of all, get it across to our host that I wish to thank him for the very warm reception he has accorded us." He paused for the relay-man to convey his compliments to Klogo before continuing. "We too are not here on any evil footing. Our mission here is very simple. Torgbuiga Ashi Aklama II, the overlord of Sakabo, has sent us to respectfully request Klogo, the brave hunter, to meet him for a very important discussion at his palace, tomorrow morning. We need to carry back to Torgbuiga your acceptance or otherwise of this invitation. I am done". Tsami gently touched the ground with the end of his staff to indicate he had arrived at the end of his message.

"Well, Klogo, so says Torgbuiga's Tsami. He now awaits your response to be conveyed to his lord and master," the relay-man said. There was a long silence. Klogo chose not to respond immediately. He allowed the relay-man's message to hang in the air for a while as he tossed the invitation from the palace up and down his mind trying to guess what could be the purpose. He looked hard into the eyes of each of the emissaries trying to see if he could pick up stray clues that could make him guess the purpose of Torgbuiga's surprise invitation. The faces staring at him from across where he sat could best be described as hard and blank. They revealed nothing. After a while, he spoke. "Tell Torgbuiga, he is my lord and shall forever remain so, till he is called into the world of our ancestors. I feel highly honoured to be invited to his palace. I shall be there as demanded. Tell Torgbuiga that," said Klogo, in a very firm tone.

"Tsami, you heard the lord of this house. He says to you to tell Torgbuiga that he'll be at his palace without fail tomorrow morning," the relay-man gave out his own embellished version of Klogo's acceptance message. "Thank you. And on that note we shall beg that you press the edge of your seat for us."

"So soon? I thought you would stay a little longer to allow my wife to prepare something for us to dig our fingers into and smear our beards with."

"Another time. We have a few other places to visit before we return to Sakabo," said Tsami as he and his two friends rose up from the wooden bench. "Well, if you say so. Permission is granted. But I need to guide you out." Klogo also rose to his feet. "When you turn to the right, you go into my wife's kitchen. To the left, leads to our bedroom. Backwards leads to the main gate, which in turn will surely lead you outside my compound. I wish you well."

As they turned to go, one of the men with Tsami stopped and turned to Klogo. "What are these?" he asked, pointing at the jaw bones and skulls of animals hanging from a section of Klogo's wall like a well-strung skeletal garland. Prominent among the relics was the dry white skull of an animal with huge curved horns. "That must be the skull of a cow, I guess, judging by the horns," the same attendant who did not want to be taken for a dumb person said.

"No, my friend. Hunters do not hunt cows. What you see is the skull of a buffalo". Klogo smiled a bit and began to wonder if it was prudent to narrate the story behind the buffalo skull. Upon second thoughts, however, he chose not to and said softly, "We hunters hang such relics in our homes as an answer to the often posed question, 'How many animals have you killed?' "

"They are symbols of his achievement," explained Tsami.

"Precisely. Those are my trophies and medals." Klogo confirmed. They shook hands again as they stepped out of the compound. Klogo wished them a safe trip back to the palace as he bolted the gates from within and walked thoughtfully back towards the verandah where Akuyovi his wife was already standing akimbo waiting for him.

SEVENTH LEG

*Ame adeke meflea dadi be woale
afi le ame bubu fe xɔme o.*

(No one buys a cat so that it will
catch mice in another man's
room.)

" What did they want?" asked Akuyovi.

"Torgbuiga wants me at his palace tomorrow morning."

"What for?"

"The messengers didn't say," he paused. "May be he has finally acquired that state-of-the-art hunting rifle he often dreams about and wants me to teach him a thing or two. I mean, loading... aiming...firing and reloading... things like that", Klogo surmised.

"Are you sure?" Akuyovi wondered in a voice filled with much doubt, which did not go unnoticed by her husband.

"Why such deep doubt and uncertainty?" inquired Klogo.

"Well, I couldn't help overhearing your conversation from my corner in the kitchen. I also stole glances at your guests as I listened to them talk to you. I must say I was not too comfortable with the other man who kept silent and never said a word throughout the period they were here. I didn't like his body language, particularly the way he kept looking at you from time to time with the corner of his eyes," Akuyovi said.

"How was he looking at me?"

"I cannot describe it, but I can say I noticed evil in his eyes. I don't like what I sense. That is all I can say for now."

Klogo smiled as he took his seat and continued with the cleaning of his rifle.

"Oh women! Granted the opportunity, a woman is bound to

see the evil embedded in the eyes of the devil himself." He turned his face away from his wife and laughed.

"Just as I expected. Very typical of your ilk around these parts. Any time a wife senses danger and draws the husband's attention to it, she is taken for a joke," Akuyovi remonstrated. "It is so because more often than not, the dangers the wives claim they sense turn out to be mere figments of their own overblown imaginations."

"Oh I see. Thank you very much. I thought the eyes that see and the ears that hear, walk together as companions and complement each other. Since you have refused to let me be your fourth eye and fourth ear, I shall, from this day onwards, keep my thoughts to myself. From today, my policy in this house of a hunter shall be guided by the principle of 'see-no-evil, hear-no-evil and speak- no-evil'."

With that, she hurried to the kitchen to continue with her evening chores leaving her husband on the verandah to continue fixing his rifle. Klogo tried not to allow his wife's apparent dissatisfaction to affect his countenance in any significant way. He finished working on the rifle, lifted it up by pressing the butt against his shoulder and aimed the muzzle at a cluster of golden akukɔ fruits high up in the tree at the centre of the compound. With one of his eyes tightly shut and cheeks pressed firmly against the top of the barrel, he gave the trigger of the unloaded rifle a gentle squeeze. The clarity of the click sound emanating from the rifle, for him, was enough sign that the rifle had been well serviced and ready for the coming hunting season.

The thought of hunting again made Klogo smile with some inner satisfaction as he lowered his aim and stood the rifle on its butt against the short parapet that served as the outer wall of his verandah. He stretched his hand for the old, rusty paraffin lamp standing on a nearby table and lifted it to his ear. He gave it a gentle shake.

"There is not enough oil in the lamp," he bellowed out as he proceeded to carefully remove the glass lamp shade.

"Here you are," Akuyovi snapped as she came out of the kitchen in brisk anger to place a bottle half-filled with paraffin and cocked with a piece of corn cob next to her husband and quickly made u-turn towards the kitchen.

"And get me a rag to clean the soot off the lamp shade."

Akuyovi did not respond but instead kept going. Klogo was sure his wife's silence meant she had not heard his request. If she had, she would have respond her usual 'Yes, my Lord'. Klogo repeated the request, this time raising his voice an octave higher so Akuyovi could not ignore it.

"I say bring me an old napkin to wipe the soot off this lamp shade."

Again, there was no response, but Akuyovi returned, perfunctorily dropped an old napkin in his lap and left for the bedroom without saying a word. Klogo smiled and shook his head.

"The cold war has begun," he whispered to himself as he smiled at the darkness that was craftily wrapping itself around the compound and its environs into its dark embrace. He continued to re-fill the lamp with kerosene. He knew too well Akuyovi had entered into one of those moody shells that required real tact and some traditional diplomacy from a man to prise her out and get her talking again. A lot depended on how he was going to deal with the situation when he joined her in bed that night. Experience had taught Klogo it was not prudent for a man to follow any woman in such a mood to bed immediately. He needed to leave her alone until after midnight when the weather had caused the bed to become cold. At that point, she would need his male cloth to cover her body fully, and that would be the moment for him to launch his diplomatic offensive towards a possible reconciliation.

Just when he had almost worked out his strategy for handling his wife's tantrums, he found his mind suddenly reverting towards the visit of the emissaries from Torgbuiga's palace.

As he thoughtfully juxtaposed the visit by Torgbuiga's emissaries with the comments and observations made by his wife, Klogo started having second thoughts about his impending visit to Sakabo the following morning. He remembered vividly the last time he had been to Torgbuiga's palace. More than thirty years had passed. It was during the reign of the current Torgbuiga's father. Klogo was there with his grandfather Logosei Dzienyo, the greatest hunter Sakabo had ever known. Under normal circumstances, whatever happened then should have remained buried beneath the sands of the past to become forgotten history, pleasant or otherwise especially since the two main actors in the drama had passed on to the world beyond. However, times such as he found himself now did not make such an option an easy one for him. He could not help recollecting in all its minutest details what his grandfather had been through at the hands of the current Torgbuiga's father, Ashi Aklama I.

Efo Kodjo Mawugbe

I

Adelatsatsae doa go la tsatsa.

(A roving hunter is the one who meets the wandering game)

Logosei Dzienyo had spent about seven Keta market days roaming the forest without sighting any animal. It was as if all the forest animals were on some form of vacation. It was the last few days before the mandatory closed season that barred hunting within the traditional area, until seven market days before the Godigbeza. That meant if he did not kill any game his wife, Mama Kaogbe, Klogo's grandmother, would not have any meat to prepare a meal for the numerous family members, friends and loved ones who would be calling at his house during the festival. Logosei dared not return home empty-handed. He decided to roam the forest one more day. He spent the twilight in the thicket around the bend in the river, where most of the animals often came to take a drink and a dip. Logosei hid himself there and prayed silently to Mawu Kitikata for some animal to show up. He waited from sun up to sun down and not even a squirrel made an appearance. It was as if all the animals had decided to undertake a sun-up to sundown fast that day.

Disappointed and angry with himself for allowing forest animals to make a fool of him, his grandfather came out of his hiding place resolved to abandon the hunting and go home with an empty sack to face the silent wrath of his wife. After all, it wasn't everyday that a hunter had to bring home game from a hunting expedition. Such was life. He was still picking his way through the prickly twines and thistles on the floor of the thick forest when his eyes caught some unusual movement some distance ahead of him. He stood still. Very still. He almost became one with the tree against which he leaned. He almost stopped breathing. He slowly brought the rifle to a firing position, aiming it in the direction of the shrub where he had seen the movement earlier on.

The foliage in the distance moved again. It was as if someone was pulling down the branches of the shrub. Logosei slowly and noiselessly went into a crouching position, straining his eyes through the foliage in the dimming sunset to catch a glimpse of whatever creature was feeding there. If only he could make out the particular tree, it would give him a clue as to which animal it was. As an experienced hunter, he knew the feeding habits of almost all the forest animals. As he often said, it was the feeding habits that made them an easy target of the hunter's rifle. "It is what an animal likes best that sends it to its death." Of course, there was no doubt the statement held true for men too. Indeed, it is what we like that sends us to our early graves, he mused.

Logosei could see part of the dark brownish body of the creature very briefly, before the leaves from the branches of a nearby tree came between them. He was sure it was the hind leg. In other words, the creature was facing westwards.

He lifted his head to study the movement of the leaves on the trees above to ascertain the wind direction. Having satisfied himself that he was not in the way of the wind blowing towards the creature, he began to crouch and move noiselessly, as much as possible avoiding stepping on any dried twig on the ground. He inched his way towards the direction that would allow him to aim at the head of the creature.

At last his eyes saw the horns of the buffalo busily stamping its hind legs from time to time to keep away the forest flies, whilst chewing the leaves of the akpeso tree. He knew the moment had come and that there was no way he was going to go home with an empty hunting sack.

He held his breath, and the adrenaline surged forth through his veins. He brought the rifle into firing position. He could still see the large head of the beast. If only it would keep its head still for a few more seconds. These creatures could be stubborn. Unless a hunter hit it directly through the head, chances were it would escape with the wound and go and die far away.

As if in answer to his prayer, the creature kept its head still. Logosei then wrapped his right index finger around the trigger, pressing the butt firmly against his right shoulder as his left hand firmly gripped the barrel. He took in a deep breath and decided to count up to three then squeeze the trigger. One…Two… The buffalo raised its head high up sniffing the air.

'Could it be smelling danger in the air?' Logosei asked himself.

It stopped eating the leaves and fixed its gaze in the direction of the nearby thicket where Logosei was crouching to conceal himself. 'What at all could have alerted the animal?' he wondered.

Then he noticed to his chagrin that the wind had suddenly changed direction. He needed to act fast else he would lose the game. More adrenaline flowed into his veins. The buffalo had not taken its eyes off the bush where Logosei was hiding. Just when he thought it was time to fire the shot the buffalo started to move away. But it couldn't move fast enough. The first shot from the gun ricocheted throughout the forest sending birds hiding in the trees off into the skies. The buffalo charged menacingly towards the direction of Logosei's hiding place. The second shot tore through the air. The buffalo, head bent low, charged blindly through the thicket towards where he was hiding intending to sweep the hunter off the ground. The experienced hunter, sensing what the wounded creature was about to do, changed his position before letting go his third shot. In spite of the three shots fired, the beast did not fall. Instead, it took off on a canter through the bush. Logosei followed its bloody trail through the forest at his own pace. He was sure the beast could not keep on running forever.

Logosei spent another night in the forest and continued the search for the wounded game at sunrise. He followed the stains of blood on the leaves and foliage where the beast had trudged through. It was past midday when both the hunter and the hunted came face to face again. It was on a farm. They had both covered a distance of over ten kilometers through the forest. The beast was obviously tired and weak but not dead. On seeing the hunter, it stood up on all fours ready to charge but Logosei's rifle stopped it in its tracks as it tumbled and fell to the ground.

Logosei then brought out his long hunters' knife from its scabbard and slit the throat of the beast. He cut a few palm fronds and plantain leaves to cover the carcass and left for the village.

As was the tradition of his people, any time a hunter killed a game such as a leopard, a lion, an elephant or a buffalo or some other big animal, he announced it by firing his rifle into the air three times at the outskirts of the village on his return from the forest.

No wonder when the three gunshots tore through the quiet midday atmosphere, almost the whole town of Sakabo poured out. When they inquired and got to know it was a

buffalo, they broke into songs of jubilation.

Pow!

Pow!

Pow!

Tu degbe zitɔ!

The rifle cries thrice
Miva se looo!
Adela Logosei da tu wuto! Come listen!
The great hunter Logosei has shot and killed the buffalo
Pow!
Pow!
Pow!
Tu de gbe zi tɔ
The rifle cries thrice
Miva se loo!
Come listen!
Adela Logosei da tu wu to!

The great hunter Logosei had shot and killed the buffalo. The women of the town who had quickly emerged from their homes burst into an old agbadza song that celebrated the bravery of their men. They displayed great ingenuity and creativity by replacing the original heroes in the song with the name of Logosei Dzienyo.

See him standing on the back of his game
He wears the crown of buffalo horns

The brave one who conquers the jungle
With his slim double barrel rifle
He never misses his target! Pow!

110

Pow!

Pow!

Tu degbe zi tɔ

Adela Logosei da tu wu to!

Pow!

Pow!

Pow!

Later, it turned out that Fo Akakposa, the owner of the farm on which the animal was finally gunned down, was demanding half the meat as of right. The Chief Hunter from Akpadikɔfe, who claimed he trained Logosei in marksmanship, also arrived to stake a claim. The man from whom he bought the cartridges and the gunpowder, on hearing of Logosei's kill also appeared on the scene, ostensibly to congratulate him but in reality to demand a sizeable portion of the buffalo meat. Somehow, Torgbuiga Ashi Aklama I, the father of the current Torgbuiga, got wind of the hullabaloo and asked that the carcass of the beast be brought to the palace for whatever controversy surrounding it to be amicably settled by the wise men of Sakabo once and for all. This twist of events did not only mark the turning point in Logosei's joy but also in his relationship with the Sakabo royal house and the community as a whole, as future events would unfold.

The carcass was carried from the farm by the Asafo group, straight to the palace and that was the last Logosei or anyone else outside the palace, ever saw of the buffalo. A month after this incident, the village drunkard, Sakpli, was asked to send the skeletal remains of the buffalo head with the horns and upper jawbone to the house of Logosei to be hung as trophy. Logosei swallowed this unprovoked insult with great equanimity and accepted what was sent him with pained gratefulness. That was the day his respect for the chief and his elders took a dip never to rise again.

Ten market days after this incident, Logosei and his wife, Mama Kaogbe moved out of Sakabo to create their own one-man cottage ten kilometers into the forest at the foot of the Gemi hills, very close to Lake Zior. He was soon joined by a few relatives, friends and later , some sympathisers.

They chose to name it *Adelakɔfe*, not only as the name of their settlement but more as an honour to the great hunter.

Even though Adelakɔfe was located within the paramount area of the Ashi Aklama royal house, the inhabitants there often claimed to be autonomous of the Sakabo royal house.

At a point in time, the people of Sakabo decided to refer to Adelakɔfe as Sakabovi, ostensibly as a way of allowing Sakabo to be associated with the commercial prosperity that Adelakɔfe seemed to be enjoying. This intention was however, fiercely resisted by citizens of the new rapidly sprawling settlement. The Royal house of Sakabo, which was spearheading this exercise, was informed in no uncertain terms that should they insist on the name change, Adelakɔfe would be forced to cut economic ties with Sakabo. This meant that men and women of Sakabo would no longer be allowed to patronise the Adelakɔfe market. If this economic threat was allowed to go on then Sakabo would be denied cassava dough, gari, *akpatogui, zomi,* salt, bush meat and some other staple farm produce.

The elders of Sakabo, upon second thoughts and seeing the possibility of hunger and starvation staring them in the eyes, quickly dropped the whole idea of a name change for Adelakɔfe. The new settlement was left alone to develop and to determine its own destiny. That issue had never been raised again. That was sixty years back.

When Torgbuiga died of hernia a few years later, Klogo refused to show up at the funeral because of the manner in which the deceased had treated his grandfather. However, he did attend the enstoolment ceremony of the incumbent because he was his childhood playmate and believed he would be a better ruler and leader than his late father. Besides, he was a man who loved hunting too and had always sent for Klogo to teach him a thing or two about hunting rifles. He saw him as a reformer. He therefore considered the invitation from his childhood playmate as a call by a brother. He once again pushed very far out of his mind what he considered the unfounded fears of a paranoid wife.

Klogo picked up his rifle and the lighted lantern, crossed into his room where Akuyovi lay snoring. He had to sleep, wake up early, and make his journey to the palace at Sakabo. Klogo shut the door, bolted it from within and went to lie in bed next to Akuyovi. He lay flat on his back facing the rafters. Somehow, unconsciously, he found his right hand straying to touch Akuyovi's body. The stray hand began to strum the waist beads of Akuyovi as if they were guitar strings.

EIGHTH LEG

Ahɔne nɔ xla fom dzifoxɔ nu hafi
Ako tso gbe me va se yevugbe.

(The pigeon had been flying
around our homes long before the
parrot came from the bush to learn
to speak English.)

A kuyovi found herself seated on the dais among the high and mighty in the Sakabo society. Also on the dais were the dignitaries from nearby towns and villages invited to the durbar to climax the Godigbeza She was attired in a hand-woven *lokpo* with colourful and intricate traditional motifs and patterns derived directly from the community's rich folklore woven into it. Chiefs dressed in full regalia danced past the dais in their palanquins. Each chief was led by linguists openly displaying their glittering golden staffs of office bearing the totems of their various clans. As these chiefs danced to the throbbing drums and songs, the crowd in their excitement cheered them on loudly. Anytime a chief got closer to the dais, he put up a spectacular display of rhythmic gyrations and body movements and hand gestures to the accompaniment of throbbing sounds of the huge head-drums for the benefit of the very important personalities seated on the dais.

Akuyovi got up to cheer with all her heart when Klogo, sitting in his palanquin, arrived at the dais. The retinue stopped by the dais and Klogo stood up in the palanquin and started doing the hunters' dance. This was a feat only very few brave people would attempt in public. It was believed that any chief who could do this dance in a palanquin standing upright must have been "well boiled." Klogo happened to be one of the few hunters in Sakabo people believed possessed such powers.

It therefore came as little surprise to many when they saw him dancing on his feet in the palanquin. The thrill it brought to the hearts of the people in the crowd was simply electrifying.

The women accompanying Klogo's entourage went into a frenzy and screamed excitedly as they unwrapped their kaba cloth and began to fling them in the air. It was precisely during this moment that things began to take a different turn.

Akuyovi saw it coming but there was very little she could do at that moment to stop it. It was coming from a tall tree standing towards the west end of the outskirts of the durbar grounds. Akuyovi thought she could recognise the assailant's face, as he pulled the catapult and let go the pebble. She knew she had seen that face in the tree somewhere before. However, she could not remember exactly where. She was still trying to recollect where that face fitted in her memory bank when the stone struck its target. Klogo gave a painful shriek of "Ao!… Me ku vɔ" and came tumbling to the ground from his royal height. He hit the ground with a loud crash.

Akuyovi woke up with a start and sat up in bed. Her heart beat had increased and cold sweat was pouring all over her body. She was completely out of breath. She heard a cock crow in the distance. She turned and looked at the side of the bed where her husband normally slept. He was not there. She assumed he had gone out to answer the call of nature. When after a few more cock crows he did not show up, it dawned on her that he had woken up early and left for the palace at Sakabo. It was most unusual for her husband to travel at dawn without nudging her with his elbow to wake her up to say a word or two before departure. She sensed, and rightly too, that her attitude the previous night might have been the cause. Akuyovi could not help blaming herself for everything. Had she not left for bed in an angry mood the night before, she would have had the opportunity to share her dream with him. Nonetheless, she resolved to do that which she thought was necessary as a wife under the circumstances such as she found herself. She faintly remembered the face in the tree in her dream. At one point it resembled the village drunkard at Sakabo called Sakpli and at another moment it also looked like one of the attendants who had accompanied Tsami to see her husband the previous evening. Yes, the one whose countenance and body language had given her cause for concern. She thought that was the face hiding in the tree. The man who shot the husband with a catapult in the dream could not have been a drunkard. To the best of her knowledge, drunkards did not climb trees.

Akuyovi did not need to consult Bokɔ Dzelu's *afa* oracle to divine the meaning of her dream. It was as clear as daylight her husband was in grave danger. If she would be able to save him, then she ought to act fast. It was possible the assailant was going to waylay him on the bush path between Adelakɔfe and Sakabo. The thought of it made her dash out of the room, pick the calabash and go to fetch water from the huge water pot buried near the corner of the kitchen.

She hurried to the kitchen, brought out the akpaku in which the corn flour was kept. She fetched a handful and poured it into the water in the calabash. With the left hand firmly holding the calabash, she stirred the flour in the water with her right hand. As she stirred the mixture to give it an even consistency, she could not help talking to herself.

"Nobody is going to snatch my husband away from me. His life is in the hands of Mawu Sogbo-Lisa, the Great One above. He alone has the right to call him to join his ancestors. The plans of evil men shall come to nothing."

She moved to the centre of the compound. She turned to face where the sun rose and lifted the calabash sky-high with both hands.

"*Mawu Sogbo-Lisa, Kitikata,Me yɔ wo!*
God the creator of life and all things, I call on you.

Kpetekpleme-tegbe-tegbe Mawu, Me yɔ wo...
God the rock of ages that has infinite existence, I call on you.

Mawu Avafiaga!, Wo ha me yɔ wo!
God the Army General, I call you

Yi ava matsi ava, wo ha me yɔ wo
You who lead us into battle and are never vanquished, I call you too.
So, god of thunder, I call on you to stand by.
Spirits of our brave ancestors, I require your presence here and now!"
She poured some of the mixture on the ground at her feet.

"Accept this dzatsi as your welcome drink and incline your ears to my supplications.

Our elders say, it is the rooster that crows and not the hen. But when the rooster is away from home the hen may crow too when there is danger.

When you hear my voice this early morning, ye spirits around,

Do not shut your ears to my cry because I am a woman wearing a man's hat.

A man's death, indeed we say, is not far. It is a woman's death that is in the distant future.

The life of the man you have given me is under threat.

A hyena hiding in a tree by the way side intends pouncing on your son.

Take this *dzatsi...*"

Once again, she poured a little bit of the mixture on the ground at her feet.

"... drink it and blind the hyena so that it shall look but not see your son pass under its very eyes. Even where it sees, let him not recognise him"

She spilled a little more of the dzatsi on the ground. "*Xebieso,* god of thunder, I offer you this drink..."

More of the stuff from the calabash spilled on the ground. "Take it, drink all of it and pull the trigger of your heavy heavenly canon to release a thunder bolt to scatter the very tree that offers refuge to my husband's assailant.

Ahoooo... Xebieso!

Ahoooo... Xebieso!

Efo Kodjo Mawugbe

Ahoooo... Xebieso!
I call you three times.
Now, go to work."

She poured the rest of the stuff on the ground in a manner that left behind a strange white pattern of a giant bird's webbed feet in corn flour. That was Akuyovi's final act marking the end of her prayer. She tasted the dregs at the bottom of the calabash and proceeded to get ready to trek up to Sakabo to check on her husband, Klogo.

NINTH LEG

Nu si avu kpɔ na wona la, menye eya kee dadi kpɔna xlɔna o.

(What the dog sees and barks is not the same thing that which the cat sees and miaows.)

Many were the thoughts floating through Akuyovi's mind as she brushed through the early morning dew on the grass and foliage along the narrow footpath that linked Adelakɔfe and Sakabo.

Who is it that wants to harm her husband and for what reason? Klogo is someone everyone in the two communities likes very much for his geniality. He is a friend to everyone, both young and old. Everybody likes his company, she mused. She suddenly let out a painful shriek as she hopped a few steps forward and stopped to nurse the big toe on her left foot. Luckily enough, there was no blood. But the excruciating pain spread through her leg all the way up her thigh. She would have loved to sit by the footpath to massage the toe until the pain subsided, but the circumstances of her journey made that option a very expensive luxury she could not afford. She limped on, cursing no one in particular but herself under her breath for not opening her eyes wide enough to spot the tree stump she just knocked her toe against. When it dawned on her it was her left foot that tripped, her whole body was gripped by an inordinate fear. She began to shudder. To kick a left foot against an object on a bush path early in the morning, when your tongue had not tasted pepper or salt, according to tradition, portended ill-luck.

It was a belief that those who thought evil of their neighbours often stumbled when walking. As far as she was concerned, her thoughts were clean. At the time she hit her foot against the tree stump, she was thinking of only her husband.

'But you kept thinking of him only in the past tense alone. In other words you had, by your thoughts, sentenced your own husband to his grave' whispered a little small voice inside her.

She stopped in her tracks suddenly and looked around. There was no other person walking the bush path beside her. All she heard was the chirping of birds announcing the rise of a new sun. Her nostrils were filled with the mixture of the freshness and decay of forest plants wrapped up in the haze of overnight smoke rising from the charcoal burners' pits hidden deep in the forest. Now, it was quite difficult for her to dismiss what she had just gone through as a piece of superstitious hocus-pocus. The more she thought about the pain in her toe, the more she felt her husband drawing closer to some danger. She quickened her steps and made her strides a bit longer. She would not know what to do if something dreadful happened to her husband. Her life would be over. She broke into a trot. Even though their marriage had not produced any child, they were a very happy couple and she would not swap her childlessness for any other man. That was a firm promise she made to him when they discovered five years into their marriage that she might not be able to give him a child. And she intended to keep the promise.

Efo Kodjo Mawugbe

I

Xedzedeatidzi madzo, tu kukue bia dzo de enu.

(The bird that perches unduly long on a tree gets killed by
an ineffective rifle.)

Ever since she first set eyes on Klogo, at what everyone
considered as one of the most memorable annual proverb
contests in the history of Sakabo to select a Tsami for
Torgbuiga Ashi Aklama II, she knew that was the man after
her heart. Most young women of her age would have done
anything to win the heart of such an eloquent man filled with
the wisdom of the ancestors. His demeanour would melt
the heart of the most hardened woman in Sakabo and its
neighbouring villages. She had made sure she had completed
her evening chores well ahead of time so she could join the
other young girls at the forecourt of the palace to witness the
contest.

Tradition had it that when Torgbuiga's Tsami or linguist died,
an elaborate ceremony to select or appoint a new one took
place at the palace. The office of the Tsami as far as Sakabo
history went had never been hereditary. Whenever a Tsami
passed on to join his ancestors, the position became vacant
and the winner of a gruelling proverb contest that could last
for months, endorsed by Torgbuiga and organised by the
traditional council of elders, was appointed as the legitimate

successor. Nobody really remembered the last time a Tsami died or when the last contest took place.

On this particular occasion, the two best contestants who had survived the gruelling preliminary elimination bouts were bound to meet head on at the forecourt of Torgbuiga's palace at sundown. Since it was a once in a lifetime occurrence, like the sighting of an eclipse, the event attracted spectators from as far as Kedzikɔfe, Ada, Kpoglo and even from far away Anexɔ. At the end of the contest, after the winner had been declared, the forecourt of the palace often became a centre of joy and celebration. It was the time for the loser, the winner and their teeming supporters to bury their differences in the celebration of agbadza music and dance. This aspect of the contest was what all the young men and women looked forward to.

It offered them the opportunity to interact freely, without any serious parental interferences, at least for once. History had it that more marriage arrangements between young men and women were made on this particular day than any other. Akuyovi could still recollect what it was like, the last few minutes before Klogo was declared the winner of the contest that year.

In truth, nobody gave the young handsome hunter a dog's chance against the much fancied, older, tall and broad shouldered Atsuga. The latter's great grandfather, Seworvi, was a revered Tsami who had served the palace loyally many years earlier, even long before Atsuga's father had been born. Atsuga was emboldened to contest, believing in the saying of the elders that there was always an alligator where a crocodile once lived. He was certain he was going to be guided by the spirit and the footsteps of his ancestors.

Klogo, on the other hand, was just a simple-looking, slim and tall hunter who lived as a bachelor at Adelakɔfe. His slimness was often a subject people never missed making reference to. The popular saying among the people of Sakabo was that the man was as slim as his hunting rifle. The redeeming feature of Klogo, however, was his near legendary marksmanship. He never went hunting and came back empty handed. His popularity spread across Sakabo and the surrounding towns and villages even as far as the coast.

She could still see the two contestants, virtually exhausted and racking the very floor of their minds to bring out whatever proverbs might be left in there.
"The cat that catches the mouse cannot catch the leopard," said Klogo and waited for the interpretation from Atsuga. He accepted the challenge and explained the proverb, giving the moral teaching underpinning it to the satisfaction of the adjudicators.
"The coward who ventures out is better than the brave man who stays at home,"Atsuga fired at his opponent.

Klogo smiled, and after interpreting the proverb satisfactorily, sent one flying across to his opponent thus, "You have two ears, but you do not listen to two things at a time."

Atsuga quickly explained its meaning and therefore had an opportunity to throw one of his own back at Klogo.

"An elder who does not practice juju is the one sent to bring herbs". Atsuga waited for Klogo's interpretation.

"In our tradition, elderly people are not usually sent on errands. However, when this happens, it means that though he is old, he has not done anything of substance to win him respectability in society. In other words, he is regarded as a child," explained Klogo to the delight of the teeming spectators and the five adjudicators.

"Can you provide the moral teaching, please," asked the most senior elder on the adjudicating panel.

"It simply means it is achievement that makes people more important and respected in society and not mere age." A resounding applause followed his explanation. Now, it was his turn to throw his own proverb at Atsuga.

"Tre me dua Tsami o" This was greeted by a much louder and longer uproar amidst the audience. Even the judges could not help laughing too. There was only one person to whom the proverb did not seem funny. That person was Atsuga. He felt stung to the point of anger by this particular proverb.

He could take anything from his opponent but not an insult upon his bachelorhood. It amounted to hitting a man in the scrotum when you were supposed to be only playing. It was true that at the age of fifty he was still a bachelor. That, however, was a choice he had willingly made himself and expected people to respect. He was therefore shocked and confused concerning how that issue could emerge at such a time. Instead of interpreting the proverb to the audience as the rules required, Atsuga used his time and energies trying to coin an equally devastating proverb not only to counter that of his opponent but to taunt and hurt him. He tried very hard, but no proverb seemed to emerge from his confused mind. The time allotted him to display his understanding of the proverb finally elapsed. The judges had no option but to call upon Klogo to explain his proverb.

"A bachelor does not hold the post of a linguist or the chief's spokesperson. This is because there are days when arbitration at the palace could drag on for hours on end. Since a bachelor normally takes care of his own needs, especially in matters of feeding, if he spends all his time at the chief's court, there would be nobody to prepare his meals for him. And the moral teaching here is that; do not take upon yourself responsibilities that will turn out to work against your own interest." Klogo was smiling now. It took quite some time for the loud cheers that greeted his explanation to die down to allow the contest to continue. Atsuga knew at that moment that he had lost the opportunity to become Torgbuiga's Tsami to Klogo.

When the cheers finally died down, Atsuga did not have any more proverbs to deliver. His mind had gone blank. It was as if his bank of proverbs had been raided by Klogo and his commandos of teeming supporters that kept swelling with each proverb the hunter delivered. Atsuga tried to cover up his disappointment with a perpetual grin, one akin to a man carefully dragging chunks of grilled meat from a long khebab skewer. Klogo seized that moment to fire the coup-de-grace, 'Adu fu tititi ko nu, menyeadzidzɔ tae o' "The show of white sparkling teeth does not mean happiness."

Atsuga was forced instantly to wipe the broad grin off his face. Those who saw the sudden transformation from a grin to anger and frustration on Atsuga's face could not help but cheer Klogo to give them more.

"Even the largest crocodile comes from an egg… When your palm nuts ripen prematurely, it is a sign of trouble coming your way… The housefly says life is made up of the future and history, that's why it washes both front and the hind legs…"

When Klogo had given five proverbs in rapid succession without any response from Atsuga, the judges stepped in, bringing the contest that had lasted four and a half hours to a close. Klogo was duly crowned winner. His induction into the high office of Tsami was slated for the forthcoming Godigbeza, only a few market days away. Klogo was swept off his feet into the arms of his teeming supporters. Akuyovi knew she was not going to see her secret hero and the object of her admiration. Any thought of ever getting closer to him faded away like some heavy rain clouds suddenly dissipated by a strong land-bound wind from the sea. The dream of ever having Klogo for a friend and may be, who knew, later as a husband, had now become an unattainable one. She walked sadly to stand at a respectable distance on the fringes of the human ring where the agbadza troupe had started playing their drums. Within a matter of minutes, the drummers and singers had successfully turned the forecourt of the palace into a big dancing arena.

Men went for women's cover cloths and tied them around their waists and dragged their partners by the wrists into the dancing arena to literally break their inner backs, to the combined throbbing, torso-moving, rhythms of the atsimevu, sogo, kidi, kroboto and kagah, intertwined with the rattling voice of axatse mixed with the intermittent wailing lonely voice of the gakokui. It was an Agbadza carnival.

At the centre of the ring, wearing a colourful jumper over a silky pair of tsanka shorts, with a long white fly whisk in hand, was Ahiahɔafe, the singer-composer extraordinaire of Sakabo.
"Hododuio!" He called everyone to attention.
"Hoooo!" came the instantaneous response.
"Hododuio!"
"Hooo!"

As if this was the cue the master drummer had been waiting for, he set the atsimevu rolling out the rhythm that was going to lead everyone into the song to be performed;
De te gin xlibe gin to gaga!
Ahiawɔafe lifted his powerful voice above the din of the motley crowd;
"Mawu ,the creator, created all things!"
The Master Drummer repeated his tune once more.

131

De te gin xlibe gin to gaga!
Ahiawɔafe knew this was the moment to let his voice sail in
solo.
"Mawu the creator distributed all things,
Some received theirs in the morning,
Some received theirs at noon
Still others received theirs at sunset.
A bird that is destined to survive shall surely grow feathers.
The time for the good things of life shall surely come
I pray to Mawu, the creator to forgive me all my sins"

He paused for a few seconds to allow the drummers and the
other percussionists to fill in the fleeting void before sending
his voice to command and ride on the waves of their rhythm.
"Ahiawɔafe says, when we appeared at the gate of life,
Ese gave to each person a unique profession
Some people came with farming
Some came with commerce
Others came as apprentices to learn a profession.
That is the manner we all arrived through the gate of life.
Yet when a brother works to acquire wealth
We all leave our various professions and run after him.
We leave behind the profession that Ese gave us
But Ahiawɔafe says, if what you do is not programmed by
your Ese,
You will continue to struggle in vain."

The men and women who formed the circle that was to
define the dancing ring picked up the chorus.

If it is not programmed by your Ese,
My brother you will struggle and struggle in vain...
If it is not programmed into your Ese,
My sister, you will struggle and struggle in vain..."

Soon, the atmosphere at the palace forecourt was charged up with an infectious live *agbadza* drumming and music whose irresistible rhythmic throbbing kept reverberating through the night and drawing people from far and near.

Akuyovi had momentarily forgotten all about Klogo, her secret hero, the winner of the proverbs competition. The thoughts of the hunter had been replaced by the pulsating *agbadza* rhythms running through her body. From where she stood, on the outer periphery of the dancing ring, she saw a small crowd of young men carrying Klogo shoulder-high and surging towards where she stood.

For fear the over-excited young men carrying their hero might get out of control and stampede everyone around to the ground, Akuyovi decided to step aside when the rowdy crowd got closer to where she stood. Within a flash, her cover cloth was gone. She shouted but her protestations were like those of the poor farmer against the guinea fowl; they did not reach far. Her cloth was gone. She tried pushing her way through the crowd screaming for her cloth to be returned. That was the cloth she had bought out of the savings she had made from the sale of shallots she has been taking to the Dabala weekly market. It was very expensive, at least that

133

was what the seamstress who sewed it said. That seamstress charged a lot of money for the sewing. And now the cloth was gone. How was she going to explain the loss to Saganago? She screamed again but nobody seemed to hear her.

The jubilant young men carrying the victorious hunter sent him into the dancing ring for a victory dance. Initially, Akuyovi thought there was something wrong with her eyes. She could not believe what she was seeing. That was her cloth. The cloth wrapped around Klogo surrounded by well-wishers as he did his victory dance in the middle of the ring was hers. It was her cloth. The initial rage that swept through her body when the cloth was snatched in the midst of the crowd suddenly dissipated, giving way to a thankful feeling of rare, inexplicable joy.

At the end of the programme, which had lasted quite late into the wee hours of the next day, Klogo thought it would be a good thing to meet the owner of the cloth in person. He therefore would not yield to the demand from his friends to hand it out to them to go look for its owner. He kept it, wishing and praying the owner would come asking for it. Akuyovi had made up her mind to take maximum advantage of the situation presented by the cloth in the hands of Klogo. She refused to go for it right after the evening's ceremony. She would rather allow it to stay with Klogo till…perhaps the next day, or the week after... or even two weeks... or even till the day he was to be inducted.

Unfortunately, when that day arrived, it was not her hero

Klogo but Atsuga who was inducted into the high office of Tsami, the spokesperson for the chief. A week after the contest, Klogo had gone to see the council of elders of Sakabo to officially announce his lack of interest in being the Tsami of Sakabo. He gave as his reason the high demands of his profession as a hunter. Much as the elders did not take kindly to it, there was very little they could do under the circumstances. That was how Atsuga, the loser, became the first person appointed to the high office of Torgbuiga's linguist without winning a proverb competition.

When Akuyovi had it confirmed from an unimpeachable palace source that Klogo had passed up the opportunity to become Tsami to another person, she decided it was time to make the trip to Adelakorpe to recover her cloth. That was what she told Saganago, her grandmother. The old woman gave the granddaughter one of those rare wry smiles and a conspiratorial wink before granting her blessing.

"Go, my daughter. I wish you well." The old woman had passed that path before and understood the cultural nuances that underpinned a situation in which her granddaughter found herself. Akuyovi thanked her grandmother for the endorsement and made that first of what was later to become very regular trips to Adelakorpe.

Her first meeting with Klogo turned out to be a very important door opener that led to other opened doors filled with great expectations and opportunities including courtship, proposal, traditional knocking and eventually, marriage.

TENTH LEG

Kokloxɔ me kpea nu na koklo o.

(The hen is never shy of its coop.)

K logo happened to be performing two different tasks simultaneously. He had been a man not used to having people help him in his compound house. His house, which years ago was only a hunter's lodge located deep in the forest, now consisted of a two-room thatch-roofed structure that looked like a village classroom block under construction.To the south-eastern end of the structure was a roofless semi enclosure created out of woven coconut fronds now withered and browned which served as the bathing area. A bit far away from this bathing area but close behind the fence that separated his compound from the nearby bush was another enclosure that served as the *kpɔxa* to the compound. It was a pit left behind as a result of the earth that was dug to build the compound. Klogo had ingeniously transformed the deep pit left behind by the builders into a toilet. He had deepened the pit further and narrowed the top by covering a substantial part of it with logs to provide a strong foothold when he had to squat. At the western end of the two-room block was a structure that he used as the kitchen.

Next to it was the hand-dug well which provided drinkable water for the house. Further down from the kitchen, a little beyond the well, was the semi circular hearth which served as a fire place for smoking the game he brought from his hunting expeditions or from inspecting his traps. At the centre of the compound was the akukɔ tree under which he often sat to relax and to clean his rifle. Right at the entrance of his compound, towards the left, was a small enclosure which served as his shrine. It consisted of a large granite rock whose original colour was now indeterminable as a result of the regular *dzatsi* and animal blood poured on it over a long period. Around the rock was the *afla* plant, the leaf of which Klogo plucked and kept in his hunting sack any day he set out for the forest believing it would bring him luck. Any time Klogo left for hunting or trap inspection, he made it a duty to first visit the shrine to offer prayers to the spirit of his ancestors. On his return from the forest he didn't forget to revisit the shrine to present to his ancestors the catch of the day. There were occasions when he had placed chunks of roasted or raw meat on top of the rock, as a form of tithe from his catch to the spirits of his ancestors whom he believed in all sincerity made it all possible. Nobody had ever seen the ancestors coming to eat the meat so served. People had however seen crows and vultures descending from the skies to carry off the sacrifice.

When it was suggested to him that perhaps his meat sacrifices were fattening the vultures and crows in the neighbourhood and not reaching the ancestors as he intended, Klogo remarked that the vultures and the crows were the messengers sent down by those to whom he regularly offered the sacrifices and added that if anyone doubted it, they could call the birds and ask them. And with that, nobody felt like pursuing the issue any further.

Klogo, having regulated to his satisfaction the intensity of the fire in the three feet high semi-circular hearth under the pile of game meat spread on the grill above it, now walked towards the kitchen to continue with the preparation of his evening meal of *akple* and okro mixed with *gboma* leaves soup.

Klogo had never been a man used to having people do things for him. His pride and self confidence would not allow that. Of the two rooms in his compound, one served as his bedroom and the other he kept as a guest room. There were times traders travelled from afar to buy smoked meat from him. It became necessary for some of these traders to spend the night in his compound and so he often gave them the guest room. Even though most of the traders who stayed overnight were women, Klogo made sure they never crossed the line he had drawn to keep business and pleasure apart as far as possible.

He would never allow any woman, no matter how well intentioned, who spent the night in his compound to assist even remotely with the household chores. He did his own cooking. Whenever he was returning home from hunting or after inspecting traps, he would carry on his head sizeable logs that he split into splinters and used as fire wood for cooking and smoking his game.

Klogo's attitude to women made a lot of the women traders and even some men, including his close relatives, feel quite uneasy about his bachelorhood. The story was told of

Dedume, a trader from Vogah who had arrived very late one evening at Klogo's house intending to buy smoked meat and had to spend the night there. Around midnight, Klogo was suddenly aroused from sleep by the noise from the adjoining room where Dedume slept. From the way the woman was screaming, it was suspected she could be under some form of attack and needed help.

Klogo went for his rifle, slowly opened his door and stepped out cautiously into the darkness outside. He leaned against the door post and with the rifle held firmly, and stealthily made his way towards the entrance of the guestroom where Dedume lay. The noise from the guestroom pointed to the fact that his guest was in some form of danger. He cocked his rifle and fired into the darkness while waiting for the intruder in the guestroom to dash out. He waited for a while but nobody came out and yet the screaming from his guest was getting louder than ever.

Klogo charged into the guest room with rifle in firing position. The palm oil lamp he had provided his guest for the night had gone off and the room was pitch dark.
"Dedume, what is the matter?" Klogo enquired.
"It looks like there is someone in the room with me" She said breathlessly.
"Where are you?" asked Klogo as he immediately cocked his rifle.
"This way" answered Dedume.

Klogo carefully groped his way towards the sound of

Dedume's voice. Suddenly, he felt someone grab his hand and drag him down. He resisted with all his might.

"What is the meaning of this?" asked Klogo in anger, when his eyes, having grown accustomed to the darkness in the room, seemed to have caught the full body of Dedume in all its nakedness, lying on the mat on the floor and trying to pull him to herself.

" Klogo, don't you do this to me. Please, come touch my waist beads at least and go away." She pleaded as she got up and moved towards Klogo.

"You come one more step closer and I will shoot you", declared Klogo in all seriousness. Dedume couldn't be bothered.

"Gunning down a woman like game. How do you explain that to the whole community when morning breaks? That you pursued an antelope into your guest room...?

"Stay where you are and don't you come any closer."

"...And you shot that antelope but when you went to lift it up it had mysteriously transformed itself into a woman. Will that be your story?" she moved closer to Klogo.

"I am warning you for the last time, you take one more step towards me and I will pull the trigger" Even as he spoke he was moving backwards.

"Go ahead and pull the trigger and become the people's hero for murdering a regular innocent customer of yours.... Go ahead and pull the trigger." Dedume was now only an arm's length away from Klogo. Klogo ran out of the room and out of his own house into the dark night carrying his gun with him. He abandoned his bed, room, and house to the trader from Vogah.

Early the following morning, Klogo returned to the house with some relatives but the trader from Vogah had long gone. Somehow, the story broke out with people creating their own versions. What, however, was important was that when the dust settled and the truth finally came out, Klogo's reputation went several notches higher. He came to be respected among his peers as a man who would never compromise on his principles.

He had finished chopping the okro and was about to put the knife through the gboma leaves when he heard the call at the entrance to his compound.

"Agoo!"

He stopped whatever he was doing, lifted himself up and tilted his head so as to incline his ears towards the entrance.

"Agoo... is anybody home?"

It was a female voice. He had to make sure indeed it was him the visitor was looking for.

"Is it here?" he inquired.

"Yes, please, I am looking for Klogo, the hunter", the female voice responded. It was possible it was one of those tempting traders who had come to buy smoked meat. Some of them tried to get their meat well ahead of their colleagues and so would call at the hunter's house even at odd hours.

"Please do enter, the gate is not locked", Klogo shouted from the kitchen.

The gate opened and in stepped a young pretty lady Klogo had never met before. He kept his eyes fixed on the young lady till she got closer to him. He did not only forget that he was preparing his evening meal but very strangely and contrary to his own nature, also forgot to offer his visitor a seat and water to drink.

"May I sit down?" enquired the young lady to the utter embarrassment of Klogo.

"Please, you may sit. How thoughtless of me", said he apologetically as he offered his guest a seat and quickly ran to his room and came back with a calabash of water.

"Here is water for you". Klogo extended to her the calabash of water drawn from the pot in his room.

As the lady took the calabash in her two hands and brought it to her mouth, Klogo kept sizing her up. She did not look like someone who traded in game meat. Then he thought he noticed something that was a bit striking about his visitor. It had to do with what she was wearing. He wasn't so certain, but he thought he noticed some resemblance between the fabric the lady wore and the cloth he had kept in his room from the night he was crowned the champion of the Sakabo proverbs contest.

"Well, it could be mere coincidence", he said to himself in a whisper.

"Thank you. The water tastes really nice. Your wife really smoked the pot very well", remarked the young lady as she handed the empty calabash back to Klogo.

"My wife?" he laughed.

"No woman does anything here in my compound. I do everything myself." he added.

"Oh I see", intoned the young lady

"Well, may I have your permission to greet you formally?" enquired the visitor. This is a lady who seems to have been brought up in the knowledge of the ways of our people, Klogo thought.

"When you bear your visitor no grudge, you do not delay his greetings and allow it to get choked in his throat. You have my permission to proceed."

"Receive good afternoon."

"Good afternoon... the people from your home?"

"They are fine"

"Your parents?"

"They are well"

"Your chickens and ducklings?"

"They are all doing very well"

Klogo at this juncture observed the mandatory customary pause to allow the visitor to steer the greetings.

"And your folks?" enquired the young lady as she took charge of the greeting procedure.

"We are awake"

"Your wives?"

This is one part of the greetings that Klogo often found a little intriguing and at times a bit embarrassing. The truth of the matter was that he was a bachelor but custom demanded that he respond to such greetings in a civil manner.

"They are all well," he said, and added, perhaps as an afterthought,"wherever they may be."

"We thank Mawu."

"Woezor"

"Ayoo!"

There was a brief silence as Klogo searched through his mind for the best way to approach matters from that point onwards. He cleared his throat.

"Well, I returned from inspecting my traps not too long ago and was busy in the kitchen trying to prepare some food to eat when you came in. It is you who have journeyed. May I know what is pursuing you, so I would know what protection to offer you", said Klogo, displaying a little bit of his oratorical skills.

"Thank you very much. Maybe, for all you know, your visitor here is rather doing the pursuing", tossed in the young lady with candour which made Klogo laugh.

"That is quite possible. As the elders say, it is when we pursue others and they also pursue us that we are able to keep the world going round."

"Indeed it is so. The observation of the elders is quite true. And they say that is why the moon and the sun keep chasing each other to give us night and day."

"That is very true" remarked Klogo and wondered with amazement at the knowledge of the young lady on issues such as they were discussing. He decided to keep quiet to let her lead the next level of the conversation.

"Well, I am looking for Klogo, the hunter". The young lady finally said.

"I am he. How may I help you?" acknowledged Klogo with

some sense of hidden pride.

"I am not here on an evil mission. I am here to personally congratulate you on winning the proverb competition the last time at Sakabo."

"Thank you"

"And also to ask you about the whereabouts of the female cover cloth you wrapped your waist with as you did the agbadza victory dance that night at the foreground of the palace."

"Could it be your mother's cloth?" inquired Klogo with a knitted brow.

"No, it is mine." replied the young lady emphatically.

Klogo had no doubt the young lady in front of her was telling the truth. She had for her top, a sleeveless blouse made of the same fabric as what he had brought home from the competition and had kept in his room ever since. For once, Klogo felt really lighthearted.

"So, you are the beautiful young lady who willingly lent me her cloth that night"

"Yes" she answered, with subdued reluctance, knowing very well the circumstances under which her cloth was acquired by Klogo that night could not be described appropriately as 'willingly lending'.

"Thank you very much, but what is your name?"

"Akuyovi"

"And who are your parents?"

"I live with my grandmother, Saganago, at Sakabo."

146

"Your father and mother?"

"Well, they are both not around"

"Travelled out of town, I guess"

"Sort of, but never to return"

"You don't mean they are both…"

"Unfortunately so."

"Oh, I am very sorry"

"That is alright. It happened many years ago when I was a little baby."

There was silence. Klogo no longer knew in which direction to steer the conversation. There was one particular question he wished to ask but seemed to lack the courage to wrap his tongue around the words. Here was a hunter who could easily wrap his index finger around the trigger of a gun and fire yet could not wrap his tongue around what his heart felt and what his soul yearned to express. He took his eyes off Akuyovi and shifted his gaze to the ground at his feet. In the soil at his feet he watched a little ant dragging along a morsel of meat larger than its size and obviously heavier than its weight. The hole where the ant might be dragging the food could be far off but with perseverance and determination the ant was sure to get home with its food. The key words here were perseverance and determination. If it worked forthe ant, it should work for man as well. When he lifted his face off the ground to meet the eyes of Akuyovi, something gave way inside him. His heartbeat quickened. He felt more blood rushing through his veins. He never understood what was happening to his emotions. He took his eyes off her face

147

and looked in the direction of the kitchen. Instantly, he remembered he had not eaten and had to prepare his evening meal. Before he could ask to be excused to go and carry on with his cooking, his visitor spoke.

"Where is the mother of the house?" Akuyovi enquired, a smile playing about her lips.

"She is not in", answered Klogo as he wondered why this particular question should hoist itself at this juncture.

"She has gone to the market, I guess"

"No", he answered but wished his visitor would change the subject.

" Maybe she has gone to a funeral, today being a weekend?"

"Not to a funeral"

"My very last guess. She is pregnant and has travelled to her parents to be delivered of a baby"

Klogo laughed and said "How I wish it were so.The truth is, there is no such person as a wife in this house."

It was Akuyovi's turn to laugh at what she perceived as a blatant lie.

"Hunters know how to do almost everything under the sun and cover it with their blood-stained hunting gear. The only thing they cannot do very well is to tell a believable lie"

Klogo was obviously impressed by Akuyovi's wit and sense of humour. He was definitely enjoying the repartee going on between them.

"Believe me, I swear by my rifle, there is no woman in my life. If there was, I would not be doing my own cooking." For

148

the first time since their encounter, Klogo looked Akuyovi in the eyes for a long period without blinking. It was as if he meant to tell the lady to search his eyes to see if he was telling a lie. Somehow, it dawned on Akuyovi that for a hunter to swear by his rifle meant that he should be taken seriously. "If you will excuse me, I'll get you your cloth and then…"

Klogo intentionally paused, as his eyes met those of Akuyovi. He was about to apply the determination and perseverance he had learnt observing the ant by saying what he had kept in his chest since meeting Akuyovi.However, before he could organize his thoughts he felt his heart jump a bit as he noticed Akuyovi staring him deep in the eyes. Was he being bewitched by the young lady or what? He could not understand what was happening inside of him. He shook his head vigorously to, as it were, shake off whatever spell he thought the young lady might have cast on him at that moment.

"And then what?" Akuyovi decided to latch on to Klogo's unfinished statement.

"Well, and then… may be… go to the kitchen to prepare my meal. What else?"

"What is the hunter cooking, if I am allowed to know?" asked Akuyovi in a very soft tone.

"*Akple* and *fetri detsi* mixed with some *gboma* leaves", answered Klogo, still trying to avoid her gaze.

"Supposing your visitor offered to prepare your meal for you… what would you say?" It was clear this offer was quite beyond Klogo's wildest expectation.

"Are you saying you will do the cooking for me?" he asked, trying to hide his excitement. If he was genuinely expecting an answer to his question it came in a non-verbal form. Akuyovi rose from her seat and crossed over to Klogo's kitchen to take charge of affairs. The hunter could not utter a word. When Akuyovi saw the chopped okro in a bowl at the kitchen, she turned to Klogo who had followed her and was leaning against one of the wooden pillars that formed the support for the shed that served as the kitchen and asked, "Which hurricane chopped the okro so unevenly?" They both found themselves laughing heartily. Akuyovi continued laughing as she crossed over to the grinding stone to grind the pepper, onions and other spices for the soup.

While the soup was on the fire boiling, she picked a bucket nearby and went to draw water from the well. She sent the bucket of water to the bath house and came back to Klogo who all this while had been at the kitchen as an observer. "Why don't you go and wash down. By the time you are through, food will be ready"

He just stood looking Akuyovi in the face. Akuyovi left him in his dream world to continue with her self-imposed assignment in the kitchen. Klogo could still not believe what was happening to him in his own house. Initially, he thought he was dreaming. In the bathroom, he had to pinch himself several times to assure himself it was real.

Indeed, by the time he finished bathing and came out of his room with a large towel around his waist with his chest and armpit besmeared with talcum powder, Akuyovi had set the table for his evening meal. "Supper is ready," she said invitingly with a smile and went back to the kitchen.

Klogo took his seat and waited for Akuyovi to join him.

"Aren't you coming to sit for us to eat together?" he asked, when he realised Akuyovi was keeping too long in coming out.

"I am full, please you go ahead" replied Akuyovi as she returned from the kitchen with water in a calabash for Klogo to wash his hand.

"Customarily, you know she who prepares the meal must first taste it"

"If you say so," she said, and drew a stool nearby and sat facing Klogo.

"Point of correction. It isn't I, Klogo, who set those rules. That is what the tradition and custom you and I came to meet", explained Klogo .

"Never mind, I shall do as custom says just to prove to you that I cannot poison you", said Akuyovi as she held the bowl with both hands for Klogo to wash his hands after which she also washed hers and then started eating. They ate in silence for a while.

It was Klogo who broke the quietude of the moment.

"Your soup is quite delicious"

"Thank you."

"I wish you could be…"

He left the statement unfinished. Akuyovi look up at him

and smiled but made no comment. By the time they finished eating and she had washed the dishes and tidied up the kitchen, the sun had gone all the way down and shadows had lengthened.

"I think I must be going now. It is quite late and my grandmother may be getting worried."

"Sure, let me get you your cloth right away."

Klogo entered his room and came out with the neatly folded cloth he had kept in his custody for the past six weeks or more.

"Here you are"

"Thank you." said Akuyovi , as she collected the cloth from Klogo and spread it out and wrapped it over the slit she wore.

"And take this parcel for yourgrandmother" "What is it?"

"Just a piece of smoked antelope thigh and some smoked grass cutter"

"Oh no. Must you do this?" Akuyovi was almost protesting.

"And why not? This is the only way your grandmother will believe that you came to see a hunter for your cloth"

"I appreciate that. I must be going now", she said as she took the parcel from Klogo.

"I must see you off." Klogo re-entered his room and came out in cloth over a huge pair of shorts. Akuyovi and Klogo walked out of the compound and took the lonely and narrow foot path on the outskirts that linked Adelakorpe to Sakabo. They walked in silence till they came to the cluster of fan palm trees that traditionally marked the boundary between

Adelakɔfe and Sakabo. Akuyovi stopped and turned to face Klogo.

"I think you have come really far with me. I can carry on from here on my own."

"You are sure?" asked Klogo as he gently took Akuyovi's right hand in his.

"Yes, and thank you very much for everything"

"No, it is rather I who should be thanking you for the time spent with me and the sumptuous dish you prepared and served."

"My pleasure"

"When shall I see you again, now that there will be no more cloth for you to come and collect?" remarked Klogo wittingly, still holding her hand.

Akuyovi looked straight into Klogo's eyes and asked, "When do you want to see me again?"

Klogo quickly let go her hand and started scratching his head not knowing what to say. Akuyovi laughed and walked on into the sunset towards Sakabo as Klogo kept watching her from behind admiring her swinging broad hips. Just before Akuyovi could negotiate the bend in the footpath that would have completely taken her out of sight from Klogo, he felt his courage suddenly return to him. He called out.

"Akuyovi!"

She stopped and turned. Klogo ran to meet her.

"Anything the matter?" she asked. "Just a small personal issue", he said.

"What is it?"

"Tell me, what will it cost a man to make an emotional

investment in someone like you?"
Akuyovi was completely taken aback by the question but
kept her composure and never betrayed her surprise.
'What type of man may be willing to make that investment?"
"Well…let us say… a hunter" answered Klogo hesitantly.
Akuyovi smiled, gave Klogo a wink and turned towards
Sakabo without saying a word. Klogo stood there confused,
scratching his head. He kept looking at Akuyovi till she was
completely out of sight.

I

Dzime gbadza me kpaa vi eve o.

(A woman with a broad back does not carry two babies at
the same time.)

The night before, Akuyovi had gone to bed quite early on
the advice of Saganago, her grandmother. She would need
to wake up very early the next morning to prepare a variety
of dishes to be served at the meeting of high profile family
members and other important guests expected to arrive in
their house A lot of the ingredients, particularly the vegetables
and the cassava dough required for the exercise, had been
procured in copious quantities from the Aveta market the
previous week.

"I hope you are aware we are receiving important guests
here a week from today" Saganago had said to her.
"Yes, Grandma. I am aware"
"Very well."
"But, Grandma, who are these visitors?"
"You will need to prepare *gboma-nyanya,* and *abolo* and
some *yakayake* apart from the *ewɔkple* and *fetri detsi*"
Saganago pretended not to have heard Akuyovi's question.
"Yes, Grandma, but for how many people?" Akuyovi
enquired. Saganago stopped and turned slowly to face her
grandchild.

"Let's say about fifteen adults, male and female. Yes, fifteen."
"Yes, Grandma, I do understand."
Saganago turned and continued walking towards the door leading to the inner chamber of the house.
"Grandma."
"Yes." She didn't stop.
"The guests we are expecting." "Yes,what of them?" She kept going. "Who are they?"

Saganago did not respond. She continued to the door, turned the handle, opened it, stepped into the room and shut the door behind her. Akuyovi's suspicion was aroused. Saganago was up to something again. It was clear the old woman had some mischief secretly tied into a knot at the end of her kaba cloth which she would let loose when one least expected it.

She resolved to do all she could to find out whatever it was her grandmother was hiding from her. That night, Akuyovi went to sleep with her two eyes and ears wide open. It was the same night Shigaye and Adukonu had arrived from Aflao and Afladenyigba respectively to spend the night in their compound. Adukonu she knew to be the only surviving brother by a different mother of her grandma's lineage. Saganago had often spoken fondly and in glowing terms of him. From time to time, traders coming to Sakabo from Afiadenyigba market brought messages of greetings from Adukonu to Saganago. There were some occasions when the greetings came with with sizeable chunks of salted fish and zomi or gari for Saganago. Uncle Adukonu's relationship to

156

the family, as far as she was concerned, was never in doubt.

Unfortunately, she couldn't say the same of the elderly woman from Aflao, the one with the crooked hip who walked with the aid of a tall crooked stick and wore some strange beads on her right wrist. Akuyovi had never heard of her name. It would be rude to go to her and try to find out in which branch of the Agblegui-Bakpa family tree she wove her nest. She decided to leave that question suspended, hoping it would solve itself somewhere along the line.

Early the next morning, Akuyovi fetched water and placed it in the woven coconut fronds enclosure at one end of the compound that served as the bathroom. She informed the guests who then went to have their bath one after the other.
She later set their breakfast of hot kɔkli porridge and roasted groundnuts on a low table under a shed pitched in the centre of the compound where Saganago often sat to thread beads. She proceeded to their rooms to announce to them that breakfast was ready. Uncle Adukonu was the first person she prompted. When she got to the old woman from Aflao, it turned out to be a whole drama.
"My child" the old woman hadsaid. "Yes,..my ...my... my..."
Akuyovi was confused as to the appropriate way to respond. Judging by her physique, it was clear the woman was younger than Saganago. She did not know whether it would be right to call her 'little-grand-aunt,' from her late mother's side or from her late father's.
"I see you do not know how or what to call me"

"Well, that is true." Akuyovi conceded.

"Well, you should have asked your grandma. Her mother and my grandfather and your late father, Midzrato, were first cousins all from the same father but different mothers."

"You mean Tɔgbui Agblegui"

"Yes, Tɔgbui Agblegui. We all trace our lineage through Bakpa to that one great grandfather. So, strictly speaking, I am your grand aunt from your father's side. Customarily, I can stand in for your father when the need arises and perform the role of a man, and no eye brows would be raised."

"I see, So, in effect, I will call you my..."

"I am also your grandmother but since I am younger than Saganago, you can simply call me Mama Shigaye"

"Mama Shigaye?"

"Yes"

Akuyovi was still not very clear in her mind whether to believe all the explanations Mama Shigaye had offered to prove where she fitted on the family tree. However, when a few more guests began to arrive to swell the number and everybody was paying Mama Shigaye one form of reverence or the other, Akuyovi then realised she was the spiritual head of the Agblegui clan. A very powerful woman by traditional standards, but quite unassuming. It was a little after midday when Akuyovi was summoned to appear before all the guests who had converged in the large space that served as the living room. They sat in two groups facing each other. One group was made up Saganago, Mama Shigaye, Adukonu and a few familiar faces. The other group was made up of five women and three men, none of whom Akuyovi had ever set eyes on in her life. On display, in the space between the two group of guests, were various items that excited curiosity. Akuyovi was still wondering what might have occasioned the celebration for which the items had been put on display when Adukonu's voice broke the trend of her thoughts.

"Well, you asked to see the one at the centre of this whole drama and I was duly asked to summon her here, into our presence. So, here she is."

Akuyovi was baffled. How did she become a central character in a drama fashioned out by the guests assembled in their living room? Could it be that someone was using her as bait on a mousetrap or a worm on a fish hook? Or, could it be part of the suspected mischief her grandmother had concealed in a knot in the corner of her kaba cloth? She looked towards the direction of her grandma. When their eyes met, she could not discern anything from the face or eyes that stared at her from across the room. The face was as plain and green as the broad leaf used in wrapping stuff at the market. It was evident Akuyovi was feeling quite uneasy as she stood in front of the guests. She started fidgeting with her fingers as she kept her head down counting her toes.

"Young lady, will you please raise your head so we can see your face."

Akuyovi obeyed the request without bothering to know who had uttered it. There were murmurings from the unknown guests when they saw the full face of Akuyovi. There were murmurings of approval. This situation increased Akuyovi's uneasiness. She felt like a commodity being sized up and priced through the eyes of strangers. She swore never to forgive her grandma for this embarrassment. How she wished someone would whisk her away from these slave dealers.

"Fo-nye, ask our friends who have travelled to our house whether they are satisfied with what they have seen?" said Mama Shigaye to Adukonu. Adukonu seized the opportunity to display whatever was left of his skills at handling words. "Well, my friends on the other side, so says Mama Shigaye, that the monkey says 'seeing is believing' that is why Mawu created him with two eyes. You came to the market to make a procurement. What you came for was not hidden in a kevi and forced into your hands to take home. You have with your own two God-given eyes beheld the object of the heart's desire of the one who sent you. Now, we on this side want to know whether you are satisfied with your purchase. Akuyovi's fears that she was in the midst of slave merchants were beginning to get confirmed. So, this was her grandmother's way of saying thank you for all the years of faithful and loyal service she had rendered to her. She was selling her off into servitude with the connivance of other family members. Raw pain seared through her chest and she felt like screaming and calling her grandma and the other family members traitors of the worst order. This was going to be one of the saddest day in her life.

"We are more than impressed" The leader of the guests from afar declared with a sheepish grin on his face to the annoyance of Akuyovi.

"Mama Shigaye, so says the leader of our friends on the other side, they are more than satisfied with what they have seen."

"Convey our sincerest thanks to them", said Shigaye.

"We are most grateful to you for finding favour with our princess." Adukonu relayed the message.

'Traitors! How could you call me princess and yet be selling me off to slave merchants?' Akuyovi thought to herself angrily as she looked at Adukonu. She developed instant hatred for the man. If she could lay hands on an axe, she would have broken his ugly abolo kpaku head with it.

"However, Fo nye, pass it on to our friends on the other side, that there is one more thing."

Adukonu did as he was told. Shigaye deliberately allowed the pause to linger on for a while. Everyone was wondering what the matter could be. The whole living room was quiet.

"I am afraid we cannot accept these beautiful items you have brought and put on display here..."

Once again, Shigaye left the statement incomplete and paused to study the faces of her prospective in-laws. She didn't fail to discern the anxiety, breathlessness and fears that had suddenly settled in between the folds of flesh across the foreheads of the guests. She seemed to be really enjoying the effect of the suspense she had created in her guests. Toying with people's emotions had always been Shigaye's stock- in- trade.

Having satisfied herself that her guests had gone through

enough emotional topsyturvy, Shigaye decided to complete her statement.

"...without first seeking the consent of the person at the centre of everything we are doing here this morning." There was a great sigh of relief and smiles from the guests on the opposite side. They chatted heartily among themselves as they concurred with Shigaye on the need to seek the consent of the main character at the centre of the drama. Somehow, Akuyovi sensed the moment she had been waiting for was nigh. She was going to tell them her piece of mind. She would tell them that she would rather die than allow herself to be sold into slavery. She intended asking for permission to visit the washroom and seize the opportunity to run away or even poison herself. She didn't care how she did it but she preferred her freedom in death to any form of servitude in life.

"So, we are going to ask her in your presence whether we have to accept your presents or not," said Adukonu, as he cleared his throat and turned to Akuyovi.

"Our daughter..." Who are you calling your daughter? If I were truly your daughter, would you be offering me to slave merchants? Stop calling me your daughter for I am not your daughter. Akuyovi's mind was running riot.

"Our daughter, we are going to ask you a few questions and all we require of you is the truth from your heart".

You are going to ask me if I shall allow myself to be sold into slavery or not. The answer is No...No..No... and No!'

162

Akuyovi heard a voice screaming in loud vehemence and defiance inside her chest.

"Yes, Uncle", said Akuyovi, as she waited for the ultimate question,
"Now, tell us, do you know any man by name Klogo, who lives at Adelakɔfe?"
Akuyovi's heartbeat doubled. This was not the question she was expecting. She kept her gaze on the floor. She was digging the earth with her big left toe and wringing her fingers"
"May be you didn't hear me right. Do you know one Klogo who is a hunter at Adelakɔfe?" Adukonu repeated the question.
"Yes, Uncle, I do."
"Good, I think we are getting somewhere. Now, our daughter, you see these beautiful items here?"

Akuyovi allowed her eyes to follow the hand gesture of his uncle. She saw two large size akpaku filled with all kinds of expensive clothes. She saw headscarves of silk, velvet, locally woven fabric and other very expensive imported wax prints. There were assorted colourful Aggrey beads designed for the neck, wrists, waist and ankles. She also spotted two bottles of sodabi and four kegs of fresh palm wine and kegs of liha. All of a sudden, something like a veil seemed to have fallen off her mind. She began to have a full understanding and implication of the episode unfolding right before her eyes in the living room. She then understood her grandma's"mischief". She lifted her head and looked in the direction of her grandma. She saw her smiling. Akuyovi smiled back and thought it was time to answer the question.

"Yes, I do" she said at last, to the relief of everyone around. "These items are from Klogo. He intends to take you as his wife. He wants to marry you. He has sent his people to come and ask for your hand in marriage. But we cannot accept their drinks and gifts unless you give us permission to do so. So the question is, do we accept the items here on display or not?" asked Adukonu. Akuyovi did not answer the question immediately. She gave a nod of the head.

"Nodding your head means nothing to us. We are not in Adoglokɔfe where we answer yes or no with a nod of the head as if we are paying tribute to lizards. Open your mouth and speak", stressed Adukonu.

"Uncle, please, I say accept the items", she said coyly, to the delight of the guests.

"Well, we all heard her loud and clear", said Adukonu, to the gathering with excitement in his voice. Akuyovi's answer seemed to have relaxed the atmosphere in the room. There was chatting intermingled with laughter everywhere. "Our daughter, you can leave us and go and continue with your work in the kitchen. When we need you again, we shall call you," remarked Adukonu.

Akuyovi thanked the gathering and hurried out of the room and away from the prying eyes of her prospective in-laws. Her heart leapt for joy. At last she was going to be Klogo's wife. She was going to have the slim hunter all to herself. She would wash for him and cook for him. She would also give him any number of children he would ask for. Akuyovi went through the day's chores with excitement in her heart. She was going to be Klogo's wife. So, this was the secret Saganago had kept from her all these weeks.

II

Agbodaze me daa nyi o.

(The pot meant for cooking a ram cannot cook the meat of a cow.)

She had had no regrets marrying the hunter and she was ever prepared to do whatever was necessary to prove her love for him, even as she was doing now. Once in a while, the thought of being childless flashed through her mind, but she always managed to assuage it just as she was doing now. At last, Akuyovi arrived at the forecourt of the palace of Torgbuiga Ashi Aklama II at Sakabo. The crowd was quite thick when she got there. She wondered what had occasioned such a large gathering at the palace on a weekday. Her inquiry revealed that a thief was about to be brought before the public as part of the preparations for his final journey to the evil forest. The evil forest was where wicked people were sentenced to serve the punishment for their crimes. According to sources, such criminals were buried alive up to their necks, their heads smeared with honey and left at the mercy of the birds of the air and other animals of the forest. It was a little after midday. The exhausted, tortured, almost breathless body of Klogo with a blood-spattered face was dragged from the palace cells to come face to face with his wife and the crowd that had assembled at the palace courtyard. The sight of the battered face of her husband made Akuyovi scream and

166

charge through the crowd towards him. The guards were very swift in restraining and silencing her and all other persons in the crowd who wanted to express any emotion likely to draw sympathy towards the hunter from Adelakorpe. The whole courtyard of the palace was suddenly enveloped in a thick silence of great uncertainty and fear.

The only sound one heard was the intermittent pitiful groans from Klogo whose legs and wrists had been shackled. He had confessed, according to the reports that were circulating, that indeed his sudden rise from rags to riches was due to golden ornaments and assorted jewelry sold to him by an itinerant Fulani trader a couple of years back. Others also said the hunter had sworn to die rather than disclose how he came by his wealth. His stubbornness had caused Torgbuiga's guards to torture him. No one would ever know that Alegeli dug a long narrow tunnel beneath the walls into the palace treasury, from where he scuttled away an unspecified quantity of Torgbuiga's valuable golden ornaments. These were jewels Alegeli had presented on the communal thanksgiving day to a very good friend who once did him a good turn.

ELEVENTH LEG

*Menye avawɔla si toa nyɔnuwo
dome lae nye kaletɔ o.*

(The warrior who breaks through
the defenses of women is not a
brave man.)

Efo Kodjo Mawugbe

"We need to act and we must do so very fast before our friend is dispatched to the evil forest," says *Alegeli*, in a voice subdued by doubt and fear. Unfortunately, he receives no response from his colleague, *Dzakpata*, who seems lost in deep contemplation.

"Are you with me, *Fo Dzakpata*?" Alegeli asks, raising his voice a little higher and hoping and praying his friend would hear him and offer the needed response.

Dzakpata's countenance is indiscernible, just as it has been since fate first brought them both together in the pit in the heart of the forest removed from any human settlement.

I

Adzido me mena aka o.

(The baobab can never be used for burning charcoal.)

Dzakpata was the first to have fallen accidentally into the deep pit. He had been there without food or water for five days.

On the sixth day, as he kept wondering how to climb out of the pit to freedom Alegeli, who was trying to rescue a palm kernel that had accidentally dropped out of his hands, also missed his step and fell into the same pit. Dzakpata could have easily made a meal of the new entrant. However, upon second thoughts, he felt what one needed most then was not food but rather someone he could lean on for support or even just talk to. In such moments, a sworn lifetime enemy could become a cherished companion.

"Stop struggling to get out. You can not get out." Alegeli paid no heed to the suggestion from his pit-mate. Rather, he became more agitated and increased his obviously fruitless efforts to jump out of the deep pit. Soon he was panting from exhaustion.

"All that energy you are expending fruitlessly to get out ought to be rather preserved and applied to the formulation of a workable strategy to lift us both out of this ignoble pit." Somehow, Alegeli thought what he just heard made a lot of sense. He stopped jumping about and turned towards Dzakpata. It was clear that raw fear had taken possession of him. Dzakpata, of course, was quick to notice it.

"You seem to be afraid of something"

Shivering, Alegeli just stared wide-eyed at his pit companion. "Do you know me?" inquired Dzakpata. "Yes, I know you." "Who am I?"

"You are *Dzakpata be deviwo me nya eku o*! The one who is quoted to have said 'Children know not death' said Alegeli, in a shrill quivering voice. Dzakpata burst out into one long hissing laughter.

"I am not going to visit death upon you. I am not going to eat you up. Relax," he assured Alegeli.

Alegeli took Dzakpata's assurance with a pinch of salt. He was not going to believe him fully. He still felt a bit insecure. He suspected Dzakpata was only trying to calm him down and strike when he least expected it. He kept himself to one corner of the pit whilst Dzakpata coiled himself up in the opposite corner. Alegeli kept his eyes wide open and monitored every move that Dzakpata made. What he did not know was that after talking to him, Dzakpata just fell asleep. It was the loud crashing sound of *Zangbetor* into the pit two hours later that rudely woke Dzakpata from his slumber. Zangbetor, in the local culture, was a powerful deity of benevolence and altruism whose presence in the pit gave hope to Alegeli and Dzakpata.

"Thank God you are here to rescue us" Alegeli said.

"Indeed, by the nature of the spirit that shapes my destiny and being, I can rescue you two easily. But who then rescues the rescuer?"

"What do you mean?" inquired Dzakpata.

"According to the laws that govern our realm, I can not rescue myself after I have rescued you. That would amount to selfish use of power. It is considered an offence punishable by condemnation into the abyss of eternity ."

"Too bad, then we are stuck here till eternity." Alegeli said despairingly.

"Not really. There is a sacrifice we can perform, to confuse any person walking within a particular spiritual radius of our location to divert his or her footsteps towards here to rescue us."

"Let's be fast about it and get all of us out of here at once, please," Dzakpata tossed in, as he uncoiled himself from his corner and slid his fifteen-foot length towards the other two.

"Well, the sacrifice shall entail some contributions from the two of you," Zangbetor informed the two pit mates. There was silence as Alegeli and Dzakpata exchanged glances.

"Could it be that Zangbetor was going to sacrifice one of them?" Dzakpata pondered quietly to himself.

"What is the nature of the contributions that we have to make?" Alegeli wanted to know.

"You will have to donate two strands of your whiskers, and your friend over here will have to provide a little amount of his venom, and I will perform the ritual just before sunrise, seven days from today."His answer put his other pit-mates at ease.

"Is that all?" hissed Dzakpata.

Zangbetor nodded.

172

"Are you sure if I provide you with bits of my whiskers and the fellow over there supplies some venom, you will not be making further demands of us?" Alegeli could not hide his doubts.

"I am Zangbetor. In the realm where I operate, honesty is one cardinal principle which must always underline our dealings with mortals."

This response allayed the fears of Alegeli and his pit-mate and gave them hope and assurance.

On the dawn of the seventh day, when both Alegeli and Dzakpata were so weak from hunger and thirst and could not even move a muscle, Zangbetor woke them up and performed his magic with the strands of whiskers pulled out from the upper lip of Alegeli and the venom drawn out of the fangs of Dzakpata. Soon after the ritual was performed in the pit Klogo, the master hunter, lost his way in the forest and found himself mysteriously at the edge of the pit. He was initially frightened seeing Dzakpata, Alegeli and Zangbetor in a pit. His first reaction was to gun them down right there. He lifted his rifle and aimed it at the bottom of the pit where the trio lay helpless. It was Alegeli and Dzakpata who started the song for mercy.

Oh you brave hunter of Adelakorpe,
Put back your rifle under your arm pit.
Level not your firepower at poor fatherless creatures
Look not at me with a squinted eye and squeeze your trigger.

173

My Father's Song

Who will tell my wife and children that
I died in a pit from the hot pellets of a master hunter?
If you still intend to send me to my grave before my time,
At least offer me some water from your bottle
And when I am strong and can stand on my twofeet You can
dispatch me with your rifle
Oh great hunter of Adelakɔfe and Sakabo.
Show mercy.

Alegeli and Dzakpata wept as they sang their plea. Klogo, from experience, would not be swayed by these expressions of emotions. It could be a ploy to trap him spiritually, disarm him and finally destroy him. He remembered a similar experience his grandpa had which almost cost him his life in the forest during a hunting expedition and the advice the old hunter gave him.

Grandpa used to share some of his experiences as he followed him through the jungle during their hunting expeditions.

'Remember who you are. You are first, a hunter and second, a hunter and third a hunter. Learn not to show compassion to any animal you come across in the forest. It is not every four-legged creature you see in the jungle that is game. Your compassion could be the path to your grave if you do not exercise it with extreme wisdom and caution. As a hunter you need your sixth and seventh senses about you all the time,' Logosei Dzienyo often said. As if possessed by a spirit

of Agoha, Klogo burst into a song in response to the plea of
the trapped creatures down the pit.

"I am a hunter's hunter by profession.

Mine is to hunt game, big and small

The health status of the game is not my concern.

My children must eat and be clothed.

My wife must go to the market

And exchange meat for the essentials we do not have at
home.

If I show you compassion and go home empty-handed Will
compassion bring me what I need to feed my family?

I ask you, will mercy feed my household?

I ask you, will compassion feed my hungry stomach? Will
compassion buy me salt when my wife goes to the market?

The questions in Klogo's song would have continued to
linger in the air indefinitely if Zangbetor had not finally
spoken

"Klogo! Klogo! Klogo"!

I call you three times.

The tortoise shell that the eagle tried in vain to lift off the
ground.

I call you again!

I repeat, you are the tortoise shell that the eagle could never
lift off the ground,

175

Grand son of Agbovi,
I call you!
Brave grandson of Logosei Dzienyo, Descendant of the
great buffalo hunter,
Indeed it is the roving hunter that meets a wandering game.
The cassava says she is always showing kindness to people
but never receives any thanks.
But what I say to the cassava is that never stop sowing those
tiny seeds of kindness and hope.
Whatever goes into the ground, if it has life in it, shall surely
spring forth to bear huge fruits.
And men, women and children shall never stop referring to
you as 'Giver of life'
Even the largest crocodile comes from an egg.
If you talk to a man in a language he understands, that goes
to his head.
If you talk to him in his own language it goes into his heart.
I am therefore speaking to your heart.
Remember the cost of the gun you are holding and the cost
of the gunpowder you put in it are not the same.

Spare our lives oh great hunter of hunters,
Spare our lives, for one day if we are unable to buy you a
new hunting gun, who knows, we may be able to buy you the
gunpowder, at least.

We three shall forever remain indebted to you
should you have compassion on us and spare our lives.
Spare our lives, Oh! great hunter"
Remember what the sages say in their song,
'Ela me nɔa klodzi dea kuku adela wu ne o'
A hunter does not to shoot to kill an animal begging on its
knees"

Klogo found himself caught at the crossroads. He did not know what to do or say. The veracity of Zangbetor's last statement from the sages was irrefutable. It was a principle laid down from time immemorial. He could not go contrary to it. Yet, he was afraid of something he couldn't place his finger on.

This was one moment in his life he wished his grandpa, Logosei Dzienyo, were around to show him which path to take. He looked into the sky, murmured a few incantations, as if to draw inspiration from some unseen heavenly entity, after which he turned to face the three trapped in the pit. He asked the trio to excuse him. He went back into the forest.

He returned after almost an hour when they had given up any hope of ever seeing him again. He carried on his shoulder a twine he had cut and woven into a sort of ladder. He let one end of the woven twine down into the pit and tied the other to a nearby tree. Each of the three beings trapped at the bottom of the pit slowly climbed up and out to the surface and to freedom. When they were all out, Klogo gave them

177

water to quench their thirst from his waist gourd. Later, they shook hands as a way of affirming their gratitude to the hunter before leaving for their various homes.

Several months after on a cool evening, on a communal Thanksgiving Day, when Akuyovi had gone to visit her grandmother at Sakabo, Klogo received an august visitor at his cottage. It was Alegeli. He had come to Klogo to show appreciation for rescuing him from the pit. He carried a large handbag and a small brownish leather pouch filled with some items. He also carried on him a bottle of *sodabi*, the local gin distilled from sugarcane. Klogo accepted the gifts and thanked Alegeli profusely for his kind gesture. They shared some of the gin, cracked jokes and ate a meal of *abolo* and *gboma-nyanya* Akuyovi had prepared before leaving home that day.

Several market days after the visit of Alegeli when his wife had left for the market, Klogo decided to examine the contents of the handbag and the small leather pouch Alegeli had presented to him weeks earlier. He dipped his hand into the sack and pulled out a metallic object. It was an arm bangle. A closer examination of it showed it was made of gold. He quickly poured the rest of the contents in the bags on his bed. They were trinkets, rings, necklaces and other jewels of pure gold. Klogo had no doubt in his heart this was going to transform his immediate circumstances. The whole world was going to see the new Klogo. He was going to shoot himself way up to the very top of the Sakabo social ladder. He, indeed, was going to be reckoned among the rich and powerful in the society. Then the rumour mill began to churn out statements about the possible source of the hunter's wealth. Some said, one day, in the forest on a hunting expedition, Klogo had come face to face with Poverty, dressed as an antelope. Before Klogo could lift his rifle and aim it at the antelope, the latter went down on its knees and pleaded that the hunter spare it. For having mercy on Poverty, Klogo was offered wealth in return.

"If Poverty promises you wealth, take a very good look at its name before accepting her offer. It is what Dede has that she bequeaths her daughter, Korkor. Poverty can never offer what she does not have. I don't believe in that rubbish," said Sakpli, the village drunkard, when he first heard the rumour explaining Klogo's wealth. Sakpli kept repeating his disbelief of the official source of the hunter's wealth to the point where many began to get convinced that the hunter's wealth was indeed, tainted with crime.

No wonder the crowd that gathered at Torgbuiga's palace when news went out by word of mouth that Klogo had been summoned by Torgbuiga to be questioned about the source of his wealth was so thick.

II

Vɔvɔnɔtɔ fe nugbedede nyo wu kaletɔ fe afemetsitsi.

(The coward who ventures out is better than the brave man
who stays at home.)

"We must act now or forever carry the guilt of our inaction
and shame on our conscience," urged Alegeli, as a last ditch
effort to get Dzakpata to give him the necessary   attention.
This statement stirred up something in Dzakpata and caused
him to turn towards his colleague.

"You have been to the cell where he is being kept, I believe,"
whispered Dzakpata.

"That is so. I visit him every night through my secret tunnel,"
said Alegeli with great enthusiasm.

"How do you see his condition?"

"Terrible."

"I hear he'll be dispatched to the evil forest where his blood
will be shed tomorrow evening,"Dzakpata said, in a tone
almost filled with misery. Alegeli nodded his head. Then
there was silence.

"I think I know who is behind this." Dzakpata said almost
to himself.

"You do?" Asked Alegeli, in utter surprise.

"Yes I do, but do not worry. He'll soon be dealt with."
"How will dealing with the culprit help our good friend, Klogo?"
"Leave that to me and Dzakpata" Zangbetor whispered as he made a sudden mysterious appearance at the rendezvous.

Zangbetor broke into a song and dance that sent him into a wild feet stomping rhythmic spin which was later joined in by Dzakpata, wiggling on his belly. They spun themselves round and round as if they were possessed by the spirit of the tigare deity.

"Da du ame-e-e-e-e!

Da du amegbetɔ vi

Dzakpata du ame

Dzakpata du fiavi Fiavi ku lo-o-o-o!

Ne fiavi agbɔ agbe

Lelotor fe ta e

Ne fiavi agbɔ agbe Alakpatɔ fe ta e Ne fiavi Agbɔ agbe a

Ahatsotɔ fe ta e lo-o-o-o-o!

Dzakpat du ame a lo-o-o-!

"Where from this song?" Alegeli wondered.
"Learn the song right away and when you go back to Klogo's cell this evening, make sure you teach him. He is an intelligent fellow. He will understand the message," instructed Zangbetor.
"What about me, the carrier of the song? Don't I need to

understand it too?"

"The wisdom of the sages is like the white man's book. It is opened and read a page at a time."

"I don't get you," said Alegeli, confusion written all over his face.

"Yours is to deliver the song to our good friend and by the time you finish teaching him, if it is the will of the gods, you shall also receive enlightenment," Zangbetor assured Alegeli and turned to Dzakpata.

"Fo Dzakpata, you know what to do." Dzakpata gave a hissing sound and nodded his head.

"Good, I go to do mine. Alegeli off you also go to give the song to our friend in distress. We shall all meet here at the appointed time. Good luck to all of us."

With that, they parted company to carry out their respective assignments.

TWELFTH LEG

Nku kpɔ nu kple to se nu ye zɔ na.

(The eye that sees and the ear
that hears walk together as
companions.)

T he midday tropical sun was high up. The earth beneath was roasting. The heat was almost unbearable. Most young girls often went to the Amimini stream in groups to swim, wash and fetch some water for household use. What they called swimming was indeed a childish game of splashing water on one another as they screamed in excitement.

Aseye, the only daughter of Torgbuiga, was returning from the riverside in the company of her friends. They were walking in a single file along the narrow footpath with their water-filled pots delicately balanced on their heads. As they walked home, their conversation often tended to dwell on boys, men, husbands and marriage. It often revolved around the latest boy to have made approaches to any of them. They teased one another and laughed hilariously through the forest as they playfully slapped one another on the buttocks.

Soon they would be entering unto the main village street into which the streamside footpath fed. Under the mango tree at this junction was where most of the village young boys often sat to either rehearse the smoking of their clay pipes or play their game of '*ave dodo*' and engage in idle gossip.

The girls returning from the riverside knew it was time to play their game. Most of them deliberately allowed the water in their pots to spill over and soak their cloths from behind.

They allowed the water pots to balance delicately on their heads without supporting them with their hands. This was what they called the hands-free style. Once the water poured on the body, their gait changed. They swung their hips and arms stylishly with each step they took and made sure their buttocks responded rhythmically with each step.

This way, the wet cloth clung and hugged tight their bodies, revealing their body contours and the slippery mounds of buttocks under the wet cloths. The well-defined outline of the waist beads under the cloth also became prominent. Indeed, the trick often worked, as it succeeded in completely disrupting the boys' game, leaving most of them completely mesmerised, as they watched their girls from behind, whilst pretending to be playing their game of marbles.

The story was told of Atakumah, whose jaw dropped and slimy saliva dripped and drooped out of the corner of his mouth to the ground on seeing those dancing buttocks. On some occasions, the brave ones among the boys would offer to help carry the water pots for the girls they most fancied. If a girl did not like the boy making the offer, she would politely turn him down but such a boy would forever endure the teasing by his colleagues for trying and failing to impress. It was common knowledge that most of the acquaintances struck through such meetings often ended up in marriages.

The girls of Sakabo enjoyed the attention their boys paid them each time they returned from the streamside. It was no secret then that regular trips to the stream by Sakabo girls was a duty they carried out with great relish.

The village drunkard, Sakpli, put it more succinctly when he said, "For the young unmarried Sakabo girl, fetching water from the Amimini stream is equivalent to fetching her future husband"

Aseye bade goodbye to her friends and branched off to take the path that led to the palace. She was about a few meters from the women's quarters of the palace when she felt a sharp sting on her left ankle, just beneath where the beads circled. It was sharp and very painful. She looked down and thought she noticed a wriggling movement among the bushes.

"It's a snake! It bit me!" she screamed.

The water pot tumbled to the ground, breaking into irretrievable pieces as the water splashed all over the place. Aseye could see the clouds in the sky slowly going into a spin. So were the trees, the houses and all the bushes around. Everything seemed to be going into a huge onelegged spin, a dance without music. The earth beneath her feet also joined the dance and was lifting itself up to meet her.
"Hold her...Hold her!" someone hollered.
"Help!..Help!" another female voice rang through the air.

Some of the girls on hearing the word 'snake' just dropped

their pots and took to their heels screaming. They had no time to care in what direction they ran.

Before the first batch of people ran to the scene from their homes, Aseye was on the ground struggling in pain. Two pin-like spots were clearly seen on her ankle. She was quickly carried off into the palace by the young men under the mango tree, some of whom had arrived on the scene in response to the distress call.

At the palace, Torgbuiga and his elders were at the tail end of the meeting that was intended to pronounce Klogo guilty. Final preparations were underway to dispatch the hunter to the evil forest. The time of departure had just been agreed upon by Torgbuiga and his elders when the commotion from outside burst into the palace.

"She's been bitten by a snake...She's been bitten by a snake... She's been bitten by a snake!"
That was the refrain the crowd that first entered the palace kept chanting.
"Who has been bitten by a snake?" shouted Tsami Atsugah, over and above the commotion of the swelling crowd.
"Aseye... Aseye!" The crowd responded in unison.

The meeting of Torgbuiga and his council of elders came to an abrupt end as all attention now shifted to the dying princess.

"Send for Hunɔga Akakpo!" bellowed Torgbuiga, after

examining the bite spot. No sooner had he finished his statement than Tsami Atsuga was seen tearing his way through the mammoth crowd that had already converged at the courtyard and was hurrying towards the palace gates and outside.

Meanwhile, Alegeli had sneaked through his secret tunnel into Klogo's cell and was teaching him the song.

THIRTEENTH LEG

Ne kese ta ago ha, kese ko wonye.

(The monkey clothed in velvet
cloth is still a monkey.)

Hunɔga Akakpo, his snakeskin bag hanging across his left shoulders,was virtually trotting ahead of Tsami Atsuga towards the palace when he suddenly stopped in his tracks. Tsami also stopped and wondered what the matter could be.

"O! Ancient One that dwells not among mortals, what is it you seek of me at a time such as this?"
"I don't understand you." said Tsami, thinking he was the one being addressed by Hunɔga.
"I am not talking to you," Hunɔga declared sternly. "But I thought you were saying..." Tsami tried to explain.
"Keep going and do not look back. You disobey me at your own peril," the priest warned.
"I do not understand this." Tsami refused to budge. He could not understand why the revered herbalist should be talking to himself in the middle of a public footpath. Could he be going crazy?
"Anything the matter?" Tsami asked, after mustering enough courage.
"I say keep going. I am right behind you. And remember what I told you. You look back at your own risk." Hunɔga roared.

Tsami knew it was best not to ask any more questions but to keep his mouth shut and keep his feet moving as instructed.

"It was good you made him excuse us, else I would have struck his tongue with infinite dumbness in addition to the fleeting blindness" said Zangbetor, from his sitting position in the middle of the footpath.

"What do you want with me Ancient One?"

"You owe me"

"Yes, I know that"

"It is payback time"

"There is an emergency at Torgbuiga's palace. I have been summoned to…"

"Torgbuiga's only daughter, the princess, Aseye, has been bitten…"

"By a snake."

"By Dzakpata."

"Dzakpata?"

"Yes"

"Indeed, *Dzakpata be deviwo menya eku o*"

"I know that children hardly know what constitutes death"

"She is between life and death, Ancient One."

"And you have been sent for, to draw the venom out of her system to give her a new lease of life. That too I know"

"Yes, it is so, Ancient One"

"You shall not do it"

"What?"

"You heard me. You will give that honour to Klogo"

"Which Klogo?"

"The one you and I know"

"The slim hunter?"

"Yes, it is him"

191

"Why, if I may ask, Ancient One"

"That is the currency in which I am demanding your indebtedness to me."

There was a long silence as the two looked into the eyeballs of each other.

"All right. I hear you. It shall be done accordingly." Hunɔga finally capitulated.

"Thank you, my good friend," Zangbetor said with satisfaction.

"But Ancient One, how do I get my anti-snake serum to him? I hear he is in the dungeon at the palace."

"Place the bottle containing the serum at your feet in the middle of the footpath where you are standing and leave the rest to me"

Hunɔga buried his right arm up to his shoulder deep in his snakeskin sack containing the accoutrements of his trade. After groping through the number of items inside the bag with his fingers, he finally came out with a small snuff bottle.

"Here you are, Ancient One."

"Put it on the ground,"instructed Zangbetor. Hunɔga obeyed.

"Now, you hurry to the palace and do as you have promised," said Zangbetor.

"I hear you, Ancient one that dwells not among mortals." Hunɔga responded, as he went down unto one knee and bowed before Zangbetor. When he lifted his face again, he was alone. There was no one there with him. His snuff bottle containing the anti snake serum was also gone. He hurried to catch up with Tsami.

FOURTEENTH LEG

Ale si Englisiawo le la, nenema ke Franseawo ha le. Ayevuwo koe wo kataa wonye.

(The English and the French are the same. They are all Europeans.)

Dzakpata and Alegeli had been waiting at the rendezvous for what seemed to them like eternity. Each of them kept wondering in his mind what was going to happen next.

"I hope you two know what you are up to. If the princess dies, we will all be in big trouble. You know that, don't you?" It was clear Alegeli was jittery and very unsure about the whole scheme designed to save their good friend's life. If there is one thing he did not understand, it was what had happened to the princess. He did not see the wisdom in Dzakpata going to sink his fangs into the princess' ankle. "I know what is going through your mind."

"Me?" asked Alegeli, as he looked round the room. "Who else is here with us?"

There was no response.

"Relax, I can assure you our friend Zangbetor knows what he is about," Dzakpata tried to assuage his colleague's fear.

"If indeed he knows what he is about, why is he not here as he promised he would? As for me, I don't want to die and leave my children as orphans," Alegeli moaned.

"Hold yourself together, my friend. Zangbetor is surely going to..."

All of a sudden Zangbetor landed from the branches of the tree under which Alegeli and Dzakpata were seated and talking.

"It is very true what our elders say, that if you mention a man's name and he doesn't appear, then death has taken him for a companion. We were discussing…"

"You were discussing whether I was sure of what I was doing, I know."

Alegeli was stunned and petrified.

"Well, if I was not sure, I wouldn't have suggested it in the first place."

"I am very sorry," Alegeli apologised.

"Never mind...but here, take this." Zangbetor handed the small snuff bottle to Alegeli and said:

"Dash back to Klogo in the palace dungeon and give this to him. Tell him, I say he must apply some on the bitten spot on the princess' ankle. He should also put a little in his mouth and then suck the venom out from the ankle when the time comes.

Now, go!"

Alegeli sped off.

Dzakpata looked at Zangbetor, shook his head and smiled with a hiss.

FIFTEENTH LEG

Bokɔ ka dɔ mekaa agbeti o.

(The diviner can foretell the cause
of your sickness but cannot secure
eternal life for you.)

❝Give way … people, give way… the great herbalist arrives… Give way please!" A clearing was made in the crowd to allow the herbalist to make his way through. The door that led to the room where the princess lay was opened for him. He stepped into the room filled with a few elders and very close relations of Torgbuiga. He saw the victim of the snakebite lying on a mat propped up by one of the elderly women in the palace. The victim was restless and nobody seemed to have any idea as to what to do to bring her some relief. But for the groaning of the victim, the whole room was engulfed in one thick blanket of silence. Hunorga stood still, looked around at the faces in the room and having satisfied himself there was nobody in there carrying any negative vibrations, decided to get into action. He held the bottom of his snakeskin sack, shook it three times, went down on one knee and poured out the contents on the floor. Out of the bric-a-brac, Hunɔga picked two leather amulets, one of which he wore over his left arm and the other over his head like a band. The latter had three cowrie shells and a red feather sewn into it. He spat three times into his right palm, lifted it up towards the ceiling and recited some incantations. After that, he spat into his left palm three times, rubed the two palms together and rubbed his face three times with his palms. He then proceeded to touch the victim's hand.

Hunɔga gave the victim's hand a gentle squeeze to which the princess reacted. Still holding the hand of the princess, Hunɔga turned his attention to Torgbuiga and the elders in the room.

"Indeed it is a snake bite. I can feel it in my veins. It is the bite of Dzakpata"

"Dzakpata!" The whole room echoed with one great voice.

"Yes, Dzakpata. Unfortunately, I do not have the antidote to that kind of poison"

There was an instant exclamation of despondency from the gathering. The faint-hearted women started weeping. Hunɔga Akakpo was the greatest herbalist in the traditional area and beyond. There was no ailment he could not treat. Whenever he declined to treat an ailment, the victim of that ailment never survived. If he did not have the antidote to the snakebite then the princess was surely bound for the grave.

"But I know one man who possesses the antidote," said Hunɔga, to the relief of many in the gathering.

"Who is he? What's his name? I'll bear the cost of his transportation to my palace and offer him first class royal hospitality and pay him whatever price he'll name. I'll offer half my kingdom, even if that's what he'll ask for, in order to save my only daughter." It was like throwing a lifeline to a drowning man. Torgbuiga, in his desperation, was ready to try anything to save the life of his only daughter. It was clear Torgbuiga had grown frantic and would clutch at the tiniest straw to stay afloat in his sea of predicament.

"Torgbuiga, the one who has the antidote to Dzakpata's

poison, resides in our town."

Hunɔga let out his words in a clear measured tone.

"Which compound? Which house? Who is he?" everybody seemed to ask at the same time.

Hunɔga refused to be stampeded by the gathering. He did not answer immediately. He owed his presence at the palace at that material time to Torgbuiga and no one else. He waited for Torgbuiga to put the question directly to him.

"Where can we find the man you speak of?" asked Torgbuiga in a voice that sounded more like a dying man's plea for mercy than an order from a king.

"Right here, in this palace" Hunɔga said emphatically.

"Will you stop the riddles and get us to the man. Don't you realise it is human life that is at stake and every second wasted is precious?" Amega Gaxa obviously was unable to hide his impatience any longer. So were many others, whose reaction immediately suggested they concurred with him. As if to spite Gaxa and all those who supported the utterance he had just made, Hunɔga simply retreated into his quiet mood and started returning his items one by one with deliberate and calculated meticulousness to his snakeskin bag. He intended this to be his way of teaching the elders and the people around that no one ever shouted at Hunɔga, the divine custodian of the knowledge of herbs, ordained by the gods. Torgbuiga, sensing that Hunɔga was going to leave the palace without mentioning the name of the person who had the antidote because of his displeasure at the manner in which Gaxa had berated at him, decided to step in to mend the fences.

"Hunɔga, please don't be offended by the way some of my elders here have spoken to you. If I or anyone here has inadvertently said anything to displease you during this short period you've been here, do accept my sincerest apologies."

There was nothing Hunɔga could do again. The leader of the community had descended from the high horse of royalty to control whatever damage his elders might have caused through their intemperate remarks. Under the circumstances, Hunɔga had no option but to reconsider his stand. He stopped collecting his stuff back into his sack and turned and gave Amega Gaxa a very hard look before turning to Torgbuiga.

"Torgbuiga, with all due respect, he who has the antidote we are all waiting for lies incarcerated in the dungeon of this palace. I am done. May I go now?" said Hunɔga, as he resumed the collection of the last batch of his items from the floor.

"Guards! Bring Klogo out at once! Handle him with care, please!" bellowed Torgbuiga, as the guards dashed out towards the far end of the palace where the cell was

located. Nobody seemed to have noticed Hunɔga stepping out from the palace.

I

Kalami dzɔ tsu mekpɔa abolo fe nkume o.

(The giant-size fried fish should not look abolo in the face.)

As soon as Alegeli heard the running heavy footsteps approaching from outside the cell, followed immediately by the rattling of the iron chains on the metal doors of the cell, he swiftly dove into a nearby hole in the corner of the cell and hid himself. Klogo was swept off his feet and virtually carried by the guards amidst his weak protestations. The cell gates were slammed shut behind them. The rays of the setting sun pierced his eyes. He could not see anything. He was unable to identify his immediate surroundings. His eyes were hurting.

"So, you would not let a man going to meet his death at midnight say his last prayers before being whisked away?" pleaded Klogo in a voice made weak and inaudible by fatigue, torture, thirst and hunger. The guards, as part of their professional training, pretended they had not heard heard him. Of course, they had not been sent in there to engage in any idle conversation with a condemned prisoner but to drag him into the presence of their lord and master, Torgbuiga Ashi Aklama II.

II

Kotɔ du gbe adeke meli o.

(There is no poor man who feeds on grass.)

The sight of the angry-looking guards carrying the hunter with a battered face skyhigh caused a lot of people at the inner courtyard of the palace to step aside. The door of the inner chamber opened. The guards brought Klogo in and gently put him on the floor. Klogo saw the victim of the snakebite lying almost breathless on a mat on the floor.

"Torgbuiga, we have brought Klogo as requested," announced the head of the palace guards. Torgbuiga, who all this while had been gazing through one of the palace windows into the outer courtyard, turned and rushed to Klogo. He bent low to Klogo's level and in a voice subdued by humility said, "My good friend, I am told you are the only person who holds the key to my daughter's survival. Klogo, you have the power to save my only daughter's life."

Klogo just kept looking down on the floor at his feet. He would not say a word, nor lift his face to meet that of his king.

"I'll give you whatever you want. Just name your price. Name anything." The desperation in Torgbuiga's voice was unmistakable. Very slowly, Klogo lifted his face off the floor and gazed directly into the eyeballs of Torgbuiga Ashi

Aklama II, his childhood friend. Somewhere down in those eyes, Klogo felt the heat wave of the treachery and injustice of yesteryear sweeping through his very system. He could still hear his grandfather Logosei Dzienyo narrating to him the story about the buffalo and how the carcass ended up at the palace and all that was given to him was the skeletal remains of the head with two horns for a trophy.

Should he rather not allow the princess to die in revenge for all the injustices his family had suffered in the past and one more still suffering from the hands of the Ashi Aklama royal house? His ancestors would be happy in their graves seeing one of their own pay the royal house back in their own coin on their behalf. Yes, he would do that. He would be the vehicle to avenge the pain and humiliation suffered by his grandfather and now himself. He was going to be the broom that would sweep away, once and for all, the dirt that the Ashi Aklama Royal House had inflicted on his family over the years.

His mind was made up. He was going to tell Torgbuiga his piece of mind and damn the consequences. Before he could marshal his thoughts, Torgbuiga interrupted him again.
"Forgive and forget the past and help my daughter. Please save her life, she is all I have. Name your price."
"Give me justice, to cover the past and the present!" a still small voice screamed loudly inside him to co-mingle with Torgbuiga's plea of forgiveness coming from the outside. The plea from the outside seemed to be getting stronger and

firmer. Klogo lowered his gaze as he listened to Torgbuiga's words.

"We want justice! We want justice! We want justice!" It was as if a group of people led by his grandfather, Logosei Dzienyo, were marching through his mind chanting the words. He lifted his head and looked round at the faces in the room. None of them seemed to be joining in the chant. The initial resolve to say what he intended was weakened. It looked as if the words of Torgbuiga had suddenly drained him of whatever strength he needed to articulate the demands of the protesters chanting in his mind. When Klogo turned his gaze again to Torgbuiga, he said to his King, "The princess shall be healed and I will name my price after I am done." A great relief filled the room as everybody around hove a sigh.

"Agreed" said Torgbuiga, with some relief in his voice as he took Klogo's hand and lifted him from the floor.

"Quickly, remove the shackles off his feet and wrists! Hurry!" Torgbuiga instructed and the guards swung into instant action. Klogo, now unshackled, crossed over to squat by the almost breathless body lying down on a mat propped up with pillows. A quick glance at the two legs told Klogo the swollen left foot was the one bitten by the snake. Klogo bent down and held the left leg with both hands. He located the two tiny pinpoints near the ankle where Dzakpata's fangs had sunk into the girl's flesh. Klogo brought out the tsigui Alegeli smuggled to him in the cell moments before the guards hurled him out into the inner chamber of the palace. He emptied a little amount of the content of the tsigui on his tongue and bent further down to put his mouth to the two incisions made by the snake's fangs. He began to suck the poisoned blood out of the ankle and asked for a small calabash into which he spewed what he had sucked. The substance he spewed was blood all right, but it looked very dark. After several suckings and spewing, the princess opened her eyes and suddenly said in a very frail voice. "I feel thirsty."

Klogo hurriedly prepared some concoction with the content of his tsigui and offered it to her to drink. She closed her eyes after drinking the concoction and put her head back on the pillow. Her breathing had now become regular. Beads of sweat instantly began to appear over her face like dew drops on blades of grass early in the morning.

"It is finished. She is sleeping. She will sweat profusely and she will survive, but…" Klogo paused.

"But what?" asks Torgbuiga.

"I don't know how I am going to tell you this, but I must say it all the same," said Klogo, making his voice sound like a man deeply worried.

"Whatever it is, just tell me." Torgbuiga declared.

'Well, Torgbuiga, in order to consolidate the healing the princess has received, I'll need to perform certain special rites that would require the shaving off of the hair on the head of a talebearer and the subsequent banishment into the bowels of Mother Earth of same. Unless this rite is performed before midnight, within the next twenty four hours the princess shall be bitten again by a snake again."

There was a lot of murmuring among the elders gathered in the inner chamber. It did not have to do with the rites but rather how to acquire the necessary items to perform it, in order to secure the princess' healing.

"Where can we find a talebearer in this community?" asked Tɔgbuiga in a whisper not directed at anybody in particular. The murmuring among the elders intensified.

At this point, Amega Gaxa got up from his corner and crossed over to whisper something into Torgbuiga's ears. The Chief's eyes popped out and turned round to give Gaxa a conspiratorial look. Amega Gaxa noded his head three times. Torgbuiga smiled. Amega Gaxa did not smile back but turned and walked back to resume his seat in the corner of the chamber, as if nothing had happened between him and his chief. Torgbuiga signaled two of his trusted guards to draw closer. He whispered to them and asked them to depart immediately. The guards took a bow and dashed out of the chamber and out of the palace.

Torgbuiga asked that a chamber in the palace be specially prepared for Klogo, for he was going to be his special guest during the weeks ahead. When he learned Klogo's wife was outside the palace weeping, he asked that she be escorted in to join her husband as special royal guests.

Sixteenth Leg

Afi mu aha mebua mɔ yina de dadi feme o.

(No matter how drunk the mouse is, it never misses its way into the cat's house.)

The coming week would mark the beginning of the annual traditional storytelling festival and Sakpli intended to represent the Sakabo community. As part of his preparations, he had come to Daavi's drinking spot to tell his story to any ear willing to hear him and buy him drinks.

"Traditional history has it that once upon a time, at the cross-roads of time and creation, there was no foot bridge linking space and time. A huge sound emerged out of nothing. The huge sound gave birth to the word *egli*. The word egli was held in awe and sanctity. *Egli* was hidden deep in the high bosom of Mawu Sogbo-Lisa, whose other name is Kitikata, the Creator Himself. Mawu and the word, egli, became one with time."

Sakpli had started his story in earnest with only few people in the bar actually paying attention. The size of the audience was not going to discourage him. "A good story is like a well-prepared sumptuous dish. You will always find people to eat it once it is served," Sakpli was fond of saying, whenever he did not have a large audience. In this particular instance, Sakpli was determined to persevere just like the main character in his own story.

"One fine day, out of his infinite kindness, boundless love

and magnanimity, *Mawu Kitikata* called a durbar of men and animals at the foreground of his palace. He declared his intention to share the glory of his word egli with any of his creatures that was willing to please him; but as you might have known by now, Kitikata never gives out anything for nothing. He abhors a vacuum. In this particular case, Kitikata set a real daunting task for whoever desired to share the honour and the glory of the Keeper of the Sacred Word, egli. Those interested were required to undertake a very special task. The Creator God offered the interested contestants one grain of maize and said whoever could draw a whole township of men, women and children to Him, the Creator with the single grain of maize within six days, would be crowned *Keeper of the Sacred Word and King of Folktales*. Those who tried and failed would not be spared. They would be beheaded. A few people came and tried, but ended up at the gallows. Then Ayiyi came. The cunning spider, with his usual nasalised accent.

"Is it true that you are looking for someone to be crowned Keeper of the Sacred Word?" Ayiyi wanted to hear it from Mawu directly. He was told what task he had to fulfill and the ultimate punishment that awaited him should his attempt fail.

"You are saying if I could use just this one grain of maize to attract a whole community of people into your palace within six days, I would be crowned the Keeper of Folktales in your kingdom. Is that what Mawu is really saying?" asked

Ayiyi. "It is so, but the community that you bring along must include the chief, his elders, women and children," replied Mawu's Tsami.

"However, take note, if by the sixth day you have not been able to fulfill the task..." Tsami made a fast sign of decapitation with his hand which Ayiyi did not fail to recognise. Ayiyi at this point became quite contemplative and started scratching his head which caused the crowd around to laugh at him. Many were those who dismissed his intention to perform the task as a big bluff. Some advised him to go back home to his wife and children. Convinced that Ayiyi had had enough time to ponder over the task, Tsami sought his final answer. "So, Ayiyi, are you going to take Mawu's grain of maize and proceed to accomplish the task or you will turn round and go back where you came from with your tail tucked in between your legs?"

Ayiyi allowed a long period of silence to sweep over the grounds so that all attention would be on him. "Tsami, with all due respect, convey this message to Mawu Kitikata, that I, Ayiyi Aplemaku, do hereby, in all humility, accept to take the grain of maize and fulfill the task. May my head answer for it if I fail to deliver within the stipulated six days"

"Well, Mawu, so says Ayiyi Aplemaku, the cunning one, that he would take your grain of maize away and after six days would bring into your presence at a durbar such as this a whole community made up of the chief, his elders, men, women and children," said Tsami to Mawu.

A messenger was sent down from the dais where Mawu sat, with a specially decorated calabash containing just one white grain of maize. This grain was received by Tsami and passed on to Ayiyi after which the former announced that the durbar was over and would reconvene after six days. Many were those who thought Ayiyi was stupid and even went to tell him to his face. Some went as far asking his wife to have Ayiyi taken to see a bokɔ to have his head critically examined. They thought his acceptance of the task was an act of bravado that bordered more on stupidity than machismo. Ayiyi would speak to no one. He asked to be left alone. He sat under a tree at the durbar grounds studying the grain of maize in the calabash he now had for a companion."

"I happened to be there that day when all these things were happening" interjected one of the customers in the drinking bar.

"Oh, so you were there. What did you hear?" Sakpli questioned him.

"I heard Ayiyi sing a song:
"Only one person can accomplish this feat
Only one of Mawu's creatures can do this
It is only one person who is ordained to do this
A grain of maize shall fall into a coop and a fowl shall sprout.
Yes, only one person can perform this feat.

The small crowd of customers at the drinking bar joined in the chorus to charge up the atmosphere.

"One person alone...

One person alone...

One person alone..

And who is that person?

Tell me who that one person is?"

No sooner had the chorus ended than Sakpli picked up the trail where he had left off.

"By the time the music was over, Ayiyi had taken off. He was heading towards the village of Koklokpodzi, a distance of fifty kilometers away from Mawu's town. He arrived in the village very late, quite exhausted and needed a place to spend the night. He approached the first house he came across that had a poultry farm and introduced himself as a messenger from Mawu Kitikata who had been sent on an errand and needed a place to spend the night. The mere mention of the name of Kitikata was enough to let the poultry farmer and his family extend the best of hospitality service towards Ayiyi. He was fed well and offered a comfortable place to sleep. But before he went to bed, he handed over the grain of maize in the calabash to his host for safekeeping. He made the host aware that it was a special grain from Kitikata and was only kept among fowls and nowhere else.

Even though the host found it quite strange, he dared not question Ayiyi and therefore went and placed the calabash containing the grain of maize in the coop where he kept his fowls. Then they all went to bed.

The following day, after breakfast, Ayiyi thanked his hosts and sought permission to depart. He asked for his grain of maize to be brought to him. The host sent his wife to the coop to retrieve the grain but the woman came back to report there was no grain of maize in the calabash. The host went to verify for himself and sadly returned with the same report. Obviously, the maize had been swallowed by one of the fowls in the coop.

"So, what do we do now? The maize belongs to Mawu-Kitikata" said Ayiyi, pretending to be worried.
"What do you suggest I do now, messenger of the Great One?" Ayiyi was glad the host was seeking his opinion on the matter, which was exactly how he had figured things would pan out.
"Well, I really don't know bu if I were you, to appease Mawu, I would offer my fattest broiler as compensation. I don't know what you think, but that is how I feel." The host after conferring with his wife bought into the suggestion and Ayiyi left his host carrying with him a fat broiler in exchange for one grain of maize."
"But what is he going to do with the broiler?" someone asked.
"What a stupid question. What do people do with broilers?" another person cut in.
"Maybe Ayiyi was going to throw a pepper soup party"

"Maybe, and may be not" Sakpli quickly stepped in to rescue the thread of the narrative from the bantering it seems to be generating into as more of the customers by then had started paying attention. Everybody was quiet and Sakpli continued with his story.

"With his fat broiler in a basket on his head, Ayiyi arrived in the evening of the second day at Egborkorpe, eighty kilometers away from Koklo-kpodzi. As usual, he was tired and hungry and required food and shelter. He saw some little boys driving some goats and sheep home after grazing in the field and decided to follow them from a respectable distance to their home. Ayiyi entered the home and no sooner had he made known his credentials as Mawu-Kitikata's messenger than the people in the house were running up and down to attend to his needs. He was served fufu with goat light soup. After meals he was provided with a hot bath and his host and the wife vacated their bedroom for him.

Before going to bed that night, Ayiyi entrusted his fat broiler into the care of his host. He made his host aware it was Mawu-Kitikata's broiler which was kept only in goat pens and nowhere else. The host had no reason to doubt Mawu's messenger and therefore went and kept the fowl among the goats and sheep he had."

"I was there that night. That night when Ayiyi went to bed, he dreamt and in the dream he sang this song:

"Only one person can accomplish this feat
Only one of Mawu's creatures can do this
A grain of maize falls into a coop and a fowl sprouts
A fowl falls down into a pen
And only one person knows what will sprout
Only one person can tell
Only Ayiyi Aplemaku can tell"

"Indeed you were there. I almost forgot that portion. Thanks for reminding me." So saying, Sakpli took back the baton of the narrative.

"The following morning when Ayiyi was ready to depart after breakfast, the broiler was dead. The goats and sheep in the pen had trampled on it and killed it. The host, following Ayiyi's suggestion decided to painfully offer his fattened ram to be given to Mawu as a token of appeasement. Ayiyi left his host, pulling a rope with a fat ram tired to the end of it."

"So, Ayiyi now had a ram" someone said in a voice that betrayed his secret admiration for Ayiyi.

"From a tiny grain of maize, to a fattened ram. Wow!" another person quipped.

"Ayiyi arrived on the third day at Fulanikorpe and spent the night in the house of the head of the Fulani shepherd clan. He was accorded a royal treatment in accordance with Fulani custom and tradition on learning who he was and where he had come from. That night, his ram was made to share the kraal with the cattle and by the following morning the cows had trampled on it and killed it. By the usual arrangement, Ayiyi got a bull from his host. He left Fulanikorpe dragging along a bid, fat bull behind him. Someone in the audience suddenly burst out:

"Only one person can accomplish this feat

Only one of Mawu's creatures can do this

A grain of maize falls into a coop and a fowl sprouts

A fowl falls down into a pen and a goat bleats

A goat dies in a kraal and a bull emerges"

The rest of the audience picked up the chorus.

"Where does the bull go?

Where does the bull go? Only one person can tell Only Ayiyi

Aplemaku can tell Ayiyi Aplemaku-e-e-e-e"

"That is very true, only Ayiyi Aplemaku, can tell what will become of the bull that followed him on a leash to the next village." So saying, Sakpli once again rescued the story from the singer.

"The next village happened to be on the other side of a long mountain range and it took some great effort for Ayiyi and his bull to climb and descend. On arrival in the village, Ayiyi noticed the people in the town were all in black. They were mourning a little boy who had mysteriously collapsed and

216

died.

Ayiyi approached the house of the bereaved family where the corpse was lying in state and struck a deal with them after they had got to know he was Kitikata's messenger. According to Ayiyi, it was Mawu who required the services of the little boy hence he decided to take him away from the world unto himself.

"However, your tears and grief have so moved Mawu that he has sent me over to offer you a whole bull so you can kill it and prepare meals for the numerous guests who have travelled from far and near to mourn with you. In return, you shall give me the corpse of the little boy to be taken back to Mawu his creator who already has his soul in safekeeping."

The elders, after putting their heads together, decided to trade the corpse for the live bull. Ayiyi had the corpse tied to his back the way mothers in these parts carry their babies. After that he shook hands thankfully with the elders and left immediately for the next village.

He has never experienced labour pains

And yet he carries a baby on his back Who is he?

He has never been pregnant

And yet he carries a baby on his back

"Only one person can accomplish this feat Only one of

Mawu's creatures can do this"

The audience as usual picked up the chorus:

A grain of maize falls into a coop and a fowl sprouts
A fowl falls into a pen and a goat bleats
A goat dies in a kraal and a bull emerges"
A live bull is exchanged for a corpse
Where does the corpse go?
Only one person can tell
Only Ayiyi Aplemaku can tell
Ayiyi Aplemaku-e-e-e-e"

"By the time Ayiyi got to Amegbetɔkɔfe it was quite late. People were about to go to bed. He sought the palace of the chief and announced his presence and credentials to whoever cared to know. He told them he was on an errand for Mawu-Kitikata. Mawu had sent him to go and bring his son from the other village and he was returning home to his master and Lord. He was immediately accorded the necessary protocol reserved for diplomats of his status. He was given a hot meal, a hot bath and a warm bed to rest his tired body. Before going to bed, however, he requested and insisted that Mawu's only child who has been asleep on his back throughout the journey should not be disturbed but made to share a room with the children in the palace. According to Ayiyi, the child of Mawu never sleeps alone. The chief and his elders did not object to Ayiyi's request. To them, it was a great honour for their children to share the same room with Mawu's child. The following morning was the sixth day since Ayiyi began his trip. After breakfast, he thanked his hosts profusely and promised to convey the unmatched hospitality extended to him to his lord and Master, Mawu. He asked that Mawu's child, who had spent the night with the children be called in so they could continue with the journey.

It was at this point that the commotion in the palace begun. The report that came to Ayiyi was that the little boy would not wake up. A herbalist was quickly summoned to try to revive the little boy but it was to no avail. Ayiyi started wailing loudly and hurling himself on to the ground and rolling in the dust to attract passersby whilst accusing the chief, his children and the entire village of complicity in the death of his companion, Mawu's child.

Nothing the chief and his people said would console Ayiyi or could make him stop wailing. Finally, the chief turned to Ayiyi."

'So, what shall we do now?'

'I suggest you find someone to embalm the corpse, get some members of your Asafo company to carry it whilst you and all the people of this village come along with me to Mawu's palace to explain to him what happened. That is all I can say' Ayiyi again burst into wailing. The chief and a few of his elders quickly went into conclave to ponder deeply over Ayiyi's proposition. The consensus reached was that the whole village of Amegbetɔkɔfe would follow Ayiyi to Mawu's palace and render an unqualified apology to Mawu in person.

It was the sixth day. Mawu was seated at the well-attended durbar. Chiefs from other neighbouring towns and villages had been invited to the ceremony. The executioners were also standing by. The Asafo drums were throbbing but nobody was dancing. The atmosphere was tense. Everyone waited for the emergence of Ayiyi. Mawu had been sitting for close to four hours when Ayiyi finally arrived with a long retinue of chief, queen mother, linguist, elders, men and women, children and pallbearers carrying the corpse of the unidentified child. He handed them all over to Mawu.

Mawu was so pleased that he declared that until further notice and from generation to generation, Ayiyi should be the sole hero in and the gatekeeper of all folktales."

"I happened to be around when the honours were being bestowed on Ayiyi," a lady who had been listening to the story with rapt attention since it began thought it was time to offer an interjection.

"What did you see on that day?" Sakpli decided to play along. I saw Ayiyi's wife and children clamouring round their father and singing:

"Only one person can accomplish this feat

Only one of Mawu's creatures can do this

A grain of maize falls into a coop and a fowl sprouts

A fowl falls into a pen and a goat bleats

A goat dies in a kraal and a bull emerges"

A live bull is exchanged for a corpse

And the corpse is exchanged for the living

"Only one person can accomplish this feat

*Only one of Mawu's creatures can do this Only Ayiyi can
do this*
Only Aplemaku can do this

Aplemaku-e-e-e-e!

The audience in the bar picked up the refrain and sang it over and over in all shades and hues and tones coloured in alcohol. Some of the people around bought drinks for Sakpli.

As he emptied the fourth calabash of the fresh frothy stuff down his gullet and wiped his mouth with the back of the same hand that held the calabash, he boasted about his connections with Sakabo royalty. It was a thing Sakpli did at the least opportunity, even as he was doing now at Daavi's palm wine drinking joint. When his attention was drawn to the long lines of charcoal decorating one side of the inner walls of the drinking bar which represented how much he owed the bar owner, Sakpli said to the palm wine seller:
"Prepare the bill and submit it to Torgbuiga at the palace for immediate settlement."
"What did you say?" asked Daavi.
"Do you have cotton wool in your ears? I said debit the royal treasury of Sakabo," he emphasized in his drunken slurred voice.

The palm wine seller on this particular day was not in a jocular mood. She suspended attending to the other customers and went over to where Sakpli was sitting. She tied her cloth firmly around her body, stood akimbo and roared in anger.

221

"If you are indeed the man that you claim to be, repeat that statement one more time," Daavi said threateningly.

"What statement?" Sakpli pretended to be suffering from temporary amnesia.

"What did you say when I asked for the money you owed me for the palm wine you've been drinking for the past eighteen months?"

"Oh that, Tso-o-o... Daavi, are you trying to tell me that you are offended? I only meant it as a joke between friends."

"I am sorry, I don't go joking for the tapper to give me the stuff I come to sell here. I pay with hard-earned cash. So, be quick. I need my money, all of it." Daavi insisted.

"Stop disgracing me in public. I'll pay you when my pension money comes. You know I once taught as a pupil teacher at Akpadikɔfe Local Authority Primary School. They say the Whiteman's machine that calculates the pension benefits has broken down. My benefits are being worked out manually... and...as you already know...things done manually often take time. So, bear with me. I'll pay you everything in full"

"Same story every time you are confronted with your indebtedness. Well, I am serving you a final notice that you are going to pay with interest," stressed Daavi unequivocally.

"Of course, with interest my dear. That is principal multiplied by time multiplied by rate all over undred and that gives you interest."

"I don't understand," confessed Daavi.

"Don't you worry. Just give me one medium size calabash of palm wine and I shall explain the formula to you."

"You're sure?"

"Don't doubt me. It is the white man's formula for making profit. That is why they are always developing. What our people have done over the years is to learn it without applying it."

"So, that is why we remain poor and they get richer"

"You are wise, my sister."

"Why don't you teach me so that…."

"Don't waste your breath. Only bring me a calabash full of palm wine and the deal is sealed."

Daavi dashed excitedly to her pot, picked a fresh calabash and filled it with the stuff to the brim.

The two guards from the palace chose this very moment to burst into the palm wine bar. They moved straight to Sakpli and announced their mission.

"Amega Sakpli," one of the guards called out.

"Speak, for your master's best friend is alert and can hear you," replied Sakpli.

"Torgbuiga requires your presence at the palace with great urgency"

Sakpli turned to Daavi, who had come to deliver to him the frothy stuff he had requested earlier on.

"Daavi, you see what I was telling you a while ago? These are messengers from Torgbuiga's own palace, sent by Torgbuiga's own mouth, to bring me into Torgbuiga's own presence. Now, you have to believe me when I tell you I have royal connections"

"I believe you, Sakpli"

"Good, now let me have the calabash"

Then he turned towards the guards.

223

"May I empty this stuff into my stomach then we can…"
"You will not" snapped one of the guards as he took the calabash from Sakpli and handed it back to Daavi.
"Oh, how thoughtless of me. I do understand. I am going to meet royalty. My breath must be free from alcohol," Sakpli said, trying to justify the action of the palace guards to Daavi.
"Shall we go now?" said the guard, making it sound more of an order than a polite request. Sakpli got off his seat and turned to Daavi.
"Sweetie, I'll see you later this evening"
"The formula for making interest on money. Don't forget," she reminded him.
"Don't you worry. When I get back this evening, I shall teach you another one called compound interest" He assured her.
"Well, I can't wait. My regards to Torgbuiga, when you get to the palace."
"He'll be informed" He cleared his throat looked to the left and right, gave Daavi a wink and a smile and said to the guards.
"Well, I am ready. Shall we?" He belched.
The leader of the guards signalled his colleague and soon Sakpli was escorted out of Daavi's drinking bar, into the street leading to Torgbuiga's palace.

Efo Kodjo Mawugbe

I

Afɔ deka tɔ me tu a ampe o.

(A one legged person does not play the game of ampe.)

Only very few people remembered seeing Sakpli that evening. It also turned out to be the very last time anyone ever saw or heard of the drunkard of Sakabo. That same night, when all of Sakabo had gone to bed, there was a bizarre fire outbreak which razed Sakpli's cottage to the ground. People said it was purely accidental. There was only one person who could tell exactly what it was. That person was Sakpli but, surprisingly, he was nowhere to be found. There were all manner of rumours that sought to explain Sakpli's whereabouts. Some said he was buried alive under the river bed of the Amimini. Some also said he was blindfolded and led at midnight by the Asafo Company into the evil forest, where he was abandoned.

There was another group of people who believed he had been chained to some heavy iron weight, dropped into the deepest portion of Gbaga to serve as food for the crocodiles. All that was left was the burnt earth showing the spot where Sakpli's cottage once stood.

Many market days had passed and Daavi and some of her

concerned customers were still wondering about Sakpli's whereabouts. She missed him so much. Anytime she looked upon the long lines of charcoal drawn against the wall in her bar she remembered Sakpli. She missed his interesting folktales that drew customers to her drinking bar.

Efo Kodjo Mawugbe

II

Axatse menɔa vu nu vu gbea vivi o.

(The drumming is never sour in the ear when a rattle accompanies it.)

Klogo and Akuyovi returned to their own home at Adelakɔfe after being special guests of the royal family at Sakabo. The good news was that something strange had happened to Akuyovi. She was two and a half months pregnant. On this particular evening, Klogo and his wife were sitting together happily after meals discussing the kind of naming ceremony they were going to organize when the baby finally arrived. Suddenly, there was a whirlwind that seemed to turn things upside down in Klogo's compound. Then Klogo thought he heard a song in the wind. It was being sung by three voices. Klogo asked his wife if she could also hear the voices in the whirlwind. She shook her head, thinking either her husband was going round the bend or she was being made fun of by him. Klogo recognised the voices as those of his three friends.

Klogo joined in the singing:

"*Da du ame-e-e-e-e! Da du amegbetɔ vi*
Dzakpata du ame

Dzakpata du fiavi

Fiavi ku lo-o-o-o!

Ne fiavi agbɔ agbe

Lelotɔ fe ta e

Ne fiavi agbɔ agbe

Alakpatɔ fe ta e

Ne fiavi Agbɔ agbe a

Ahatsotɔ fe ta e lo-o-o-o-o!

Dzakpata du ame lo-o-o-.

His wife looked on, completely bemused.

"Where from that song?" She asked her husband.

For an answer, Klogo just kept singing as the whirlwind gently abated. He knew it was his three friends, who had called to wish him well. Akuyovi stood watching her husband sing. She could not hear the voices of the full quartet. She could only hear the lone voice of her husband, Klogo, the brave slim hunter of Sakabo.

"Da du ame-e-e-e-e! Da du amegbetɔ vi

Dzakpata du ame

Dzakpata du fiavi Fiavi ku lo-o-o-o!

GLOSSARY OF SOME INDEGENOUS WORDS AND PHRASES

Abɔbi ~ Anchovies

Abɔdzokpo ~ Kindergarten or nursery school

Abolo ~ A meal prepared from steamed and refined corn dough.

Adzido ~ Baobab tree

Afa ~ Known in certain West African countries as *Ifa*. It is an oracle for divination.

Agbadza ~ Traditional Ewe dance/ the music that accompanies it.

Ahenma ~ Locally-made sandals from leather.

Akpadiviwoe midzrado, Maria gbɔna! ~ Children of Akpadikɔfe, get ready, Maria is coming!

Akpaku ~ Huge calabash receptacle in which valuables are kept.

Akpase ~ Juju money

Akpatogui ~ Salted dry fish

Akple ~ A meal prepared from corn dough.

Akpledatsi ~ Kneading stick used for preparing *akple*.

Akukɔ ~ Sweet sop fruit

Alilɔ~ Tiny, dangerous red ants

Ao meku vor ~ A cry of despair. Ao, I am dead

Asafo ~ The organised warriors made up of the youth whose duty is to defend the community.

Avu-koklo (Dog-fowl) ~ A double-barreled but often lighthearted insult among the Ewes.

229

Axatse ~ The rattle
Ayoo! ~ Affirmative response
Bɔbi tadi ~ A dish of fried anchovies in ground pepper and tomato.
Bokɔ~Fetish priest
Dzatsi ~ Mixture of corn flour and water; used mostly for libation prayers among the Ewes.
Dzɔgbese Lisa ~ Creator of faith.
Dzɔgbese/ Ese ~ Destiny
Efɔ gbɔme fu ~ She is pregnant out of wedlock
Egli ne va!~ Let the story come
Ewɔkple ~ A meal prepared from corn flour
Ezii kpui ~ Short stem smoking pipe
Fo nye ~ My brother
Fufu ~ A popular diet made from pounded cassava mixed with plantain or yam or cocoyam and eaten with soup.
Funyetɔwo ta ~ Because of my enemies
Ga madigbe ~ The day the bell did not toll
Gari ~ Granular powder made from grated and dried-fried cassava
Gboma / gboma nyanya ~ Special spinach delicacy
Hebieso/ So ~ God of thunder and lightening.
Kidi, Kaga, Sogo, Kroboto and *Atsimevu* ~ The five sets of drums that normally make up the *Agbadza* ensemble.
Kɔkli ~ Rocky porridge made from dry corn dough
Kpetekpleme ~ One of the appellations of God
Kpɔvi... ~ Conclave
Kpɔxa ~ Place of convenience/toilet
Liha ~ Beverage brewed from maize

Lokpo ~ Locally-woven rich cloth

Maria, Yehowa ne kplɔ wo dedie ~ Maria, God lead you safely

Mawu ~ The name of God

Miawoezor kakakaka ~ Very much welcome

Mile devia ~ Hold the child

Mise egli lo ~ Call for attention to start a storytelling session.

Nade tso dzi gbɔna loo! ~ Something is coming from the sky

Ne meyi tɔnye madzɔ o ~ When I go, I will not be found innocent

Nukae mida? ~ What have you cooked?

Nyemeyi vɔnuti la dome o ~ I am not going under tree of judgement.

Sakpli eto goboo... ~ Sakpli with huge ears like a trough.

Sakpli eto lakpa... ~ Sakpli with large ears

Sakpli/Sakplitor ~ Tale bearing/ Tale bearer.

Sodabi /Akpeteshie ~ Locally-brewed gin from palm wine or sugarcane.

Sogbo-lisa/ Kitikata ~ Appellations of God

Taflatse ~ An apologetic term used before saying something unpleasant; Excuse me

Tigare ~ A popular West African deity

Togbato ~ Tsetsefly

Tre me dua Tsami o ~ A single man does not occupy the position of linguist

Tsigui ~ Snuff bottle

Tsitsiawo ~ The sages

Tuutuu... gbɔvi ~ A popular Ewe lullaby

Vɔnuti la dome ~ The tree of judgement

Wo menya 'mekae doe o ~ No one knows who is responsible
Wuya-wuya ~ With reckless abandon.
Yakayake ~ Steamed meal made from grated cassava
Zomi ~ Special palm oil that originates from Eweland

Printed in the United States
By Bookmasters